Bayou Grisé
Sins of Sanite

A Blood of My Blood Novel

C.D. Hussey Leslie Fear

Copyright © 2015 Fear·Hussey
All rights reserved.
ISBN: 1511847611
ISBN-13: 978-1511847612

CHAPTER ONE

Like a ghostly white wraith, her blond hair and chemise a stark contrast against the murky Mississippi River water, the body of a woman Sanite would have gleefully throttled with her bare hands bobbed silently on the gentle waves feet below the dock. Sanite felt nothing but vindication as she watched the body continuously bump against the pier. Over and over and over and over.

She deserved her fate. The woman who killed her brother.

Oh, Laurent...

Tears strangled her throat, choking her, robbing the air from her lungs. If she could have killed the woman a thousand times over, it wouldn't be enough to satisfy her vengeance. More. She needed more.

"I curse you," she repeated to the woman floating face-first in the river. "Even in death you will have no rest. Your kin will know no peace. As you have ruined my family so shall yours. You will walk this earth until the blood of your blood is spilled upon your grave."

Sanite would make good on those words. Even if it was the last thing she did, she would not fail Laurent in this. If it took her dying breath, she would avenge him. And she knew exactly where she needed to begin.

Julien's head was a lead-filled balloon smashing his shoulders as he took in the impossible task of sorting, dividing, and trying to decide which possessions of Grandmere's to keep, sell, or trash. Her bedroom was filled with so many knickknacks, statues, books, bottles of oils, jars of herbs, and creaky looking furniture, it was a daunting task.

She'd never been a healthy woman, but her death was so sudden, so shocking. There had been no warning—blood clot straight to the heart. He'd always assumed the family matriarch too stubborn to let death take her. The rock of the family for so long, it was hard to accept.

His brother was definitely having a hard go of it. And their mother was too scattered to focus on anything besides putting one foot in front of the other, and even that line was stumbling. But not only did Xavier have Lottie to lean on, he was the perfect son/grandson—always had been. So while he might be struggling emotionally, he still stepped up (Like he always did. Like he'd *always* done.), and had handled all the details of Grandmere's funeral, wake, and of course, the day to day business operations of Villere House.

But even *Superboy* had his limits, and the task of preparing Grandmere's things for the estate sale fell on Julien.

Not that he minded. Not really. It was the one task he probably couldn't fuck up. The rest had zero guarantees, especially when compared to perfect Xavier.

As the eldest son, Julien should be the one taking care of the family. But no, he'd been so screwed up after their father skipped town, he couldn't get shit right—except partying. When it came to tearing up the town, he was a fucking rock star. And as a result, his little brother had been relegated to alpha male long before the little shit had pubes.

The box springs groaned as he sat on the bed, sinking excessively low. Lifting the crocheted mess of brightly colored flowers Grandmere used as a comforter, he bent over to check it out. Sure enough, the antiquated mattress sat on a rusty set of metal springs. Thing must have been fifty years old. Probably the first mattress set she ever bought with Grandpere. Hell, it was probably a wedding gift.

Stubborn old coot. Why she wouldn't buy a new bed when this one was clearly worn out was exactly what made her so lovable and so incorrigible at the same time.

Their relationship had always been complicated. While their ties to Voodoo often brought them together, she was clearly disappointed in him as a man. Not that anyone ever met her expectations, not even Xavier. But while his little brother coddled her, Julien respected her power and her wishes as an independent woman. No, she didn't always make the best choices regarding her health, and no, she didn't always take her medicine. But she was a grown ass adult—not some child to be cared for, as Xavier seemed to think. She'd always respected Julien for that even if she made it clear she thought him a fuck-up.

Over the last several months their relationship had been especially strained. Even though he couldn't remember most of what happened during the unfortunate week Lottie decided to "Spring Break" in their hometown, he was still plagued by nightmares—angry, dirty, horrifying thoughts reeking of putrid hatred. And learning about the details of what he'd done while...*possessed*, or whatever the fuck it was...left him even more disgusted with himself than he had ever been. And that was saying a lot.

Shit, he'd slit Lottie's throat in the middle of St. Louis Cemetery No. 1. He'd punched out his brother at one of the local bars. It was not surprise that instead of bringing them together, their common tie to Sanite Villere and any shared experiences had actually driven a wedge between them.

Julien was still coming to terms with all of it—and failing miserably—and had taken a step back from his Voodoo roots. Grandmere, as always, embraced their heritage. She'd been extremely angry over his desire to separate himself from the horrible things he—or rather, Sanite—had done. She was even angrier when he halted progress on the book he was writing highlighting their family history and influence of New Orleans Voodoo.

"You cannot deny your legacy just because it makes you uncomfortable," she had said. "This family must embrace our ancestors for the powerful Houngans and Mambos they were. Write your damn book, boy. Make sure the world knows the Villere name. Marie Laveau can't hog all the glory."

Could he write that book now? After everything that had happened, could he venture back into the world of Sanite Villere and write about the history of the woman that made his family?

He glanced around the cluttered room. Every item, every knickknack, reeked of a heritage he was suddenly trying to escape. A heritage he had once embraced with as much passion Grandmere did. How could he deny it now? With the passing of the great matriarch of their family, how could he *possibly* deny it?

Slumping, he sighed. He couldn't. He shouldn't. He wouldn't.

But first, he had a task to accomplish.

Or many tasks, as the case may be.

He decided to start with what seemed like the easiest place in terms of sorting—the closet. No reason the fam needed to keep the clothing of an overweight old woman. As far as Julien was concerned, it could all go to the thrift store and *they* could decide what to trash and what to sell.

The bed seemed to groan in relief as he rose to retrieve a trash bag, giving a little squeak of happiness at the end. He moved to the closet, crammed full of colorful fabric, and began stuffing the bag. It wasn't long before he filled it, and another, and another. He was midway through the fourth bag before the closet finally began to look like he'd actually removed something. And that's when he saw it. Or rather, them.

Altars. Two altars. Wedged into the back corner of the tiny closet, adorned with candles, beads, dolls, and the bones of some small animal. In the center of each altar, two yellowed pictures sat in tarnished metal frames.

His throat caught. The altars were what gave their ancestors power, what gave Sanite power. Xavier had torn down Sanite's main altar, but obviously Grandmere had built another and hidden it here in her closet.

Or had she?

He almost hated to examine the portraits, afraid of what, or who, he might find. Afraid of the emotions and bits of memories he might relive if he gazed upon the face of Sanite Villere. He relived those things too often in his nightmares.

He was two seconds away from shoving the items into the bag without looking at them, ready to toss them out with the trash, until he realized the portraits were photos, not paintings.

Plucking them from the altars, he moved into the bedroom where the light was better in order to get a better look. Definitely photos and not paintings, and definitely not Sanite or Laurent Villere.

Though there might be *some* family resemblance. Mostly in the eyes and high cheekbones, maybe a little in the nose. It was hard to tell. The fair skin and light colored hair was throwing him for a loop.

Not that it meant anything. His own hair was so light it was nearly blond and his eyes were green. But that was from years of mish-mashing races—

recessive genes and all. Judging from the clothing, these photos looked to be from the mid-nineteenth century.

They were of two separate, but obviously related, women posed beside a grand, ornate staircase, wearing the typical flat-faced expressions of early photographs and clothing that looked to be of exceptional quality.

Why would Grandmere have altars for these very Caucasian looking people?

Very carefully, he removed one of the photos from its frame and flipped it over. Just as he expected, a name and date were written on the back in faded cursive. Every old photo had their details preserved somewhere in ink. But it made sense. It wasn't like they could change the file name on a computer.

Sophie Grisé 1840

Grisé... Where had he heard that name?

The other photo yielded the same last name and date.

Pulling out his phone, he opened the browser and typed in the name. Ah, that's where he'd heard it before. Plantation Grisé, located about an hour and a half west of New Orleans, was an old antebellum plantation, now operating as a bed and breakfast/wedding reception hall. That might explain the name, but it hardly explained anything else.

The only way it made any sense for Grandmere to have an altar dedicated to them is if these Grisé women were somehow tied to the Villere family.

The door opened abruptly and Xavier poked his head inside. Eyes swollen, he looked like he'd had an allergic reaction to life. Julien quickly and discretely slipped the photos into his shirt pocket.

"How's everything going?" Xavier asked, leaning against the door. His voice was thick, like his throat was as swollen as his eyelids.

"Good. There's a lot of shit in here. I may have scratched the surface." He glanced around the room. "With a toothpick."

Lottie's head appeared under Xavier's arm. "Want some help?"

Every muscle in Julien's body tensed. She'd been living there two months, and he still had the same reaction every time he saw her. Uncomfortable didn't begin to explain how the skin attached to his muscles felt.

She didn't wait for his reply. Slipping between Xavier's body and the doorjamb, she pretty much bounded into the cluttered room. "Where do I start?"

He could tell by Xavier's expression that he shared his brother's discomfort. Not Lottie though. Despite the fact that Julien had tried to kill her—albeit not of his own free will—she always seemed perfectly comfortable in his presence.

In fact, she seemed to find ways to bring them together. Like now. No way was this Xavier's idea.

He got what she was trying to do, he really did. But he hated every fucking second of it. Hated the shame he felt when she smiled at him with those big blue eyes. Hated the shame in general.

"Naw, I gotta system. Probably too complicated for you, Blondie."

She glanced at the few overfull trash bags he'd managed to fill. "You mean the 'cram everything into a garbage bag' system?"

Grabbing her shoulders, he physically spun her and walked her back to the door and to Xavier, who had a huge frown planted on his face.

"That's the one," he said.

She dug in her heels. "Julien, c'mon. Just let me help. I want to help."

"No thanks."

She groaned. "Good grief, just—"

"Lottie." Xavier took her arm and pulled her gently into the hallway. "Let's go. He seems to have everything under control..."

"Yeah right." She turned back toward the room. "Are you sure?"

"Yep," Julien snipped, closing the door on their faces. This time he was smart and locked the door.

He shook off the self-loathing she stirred within him. He was no a stranger to self-loathing, he was just really damn good at shoving it under a blanket of booze and false bravado. Not only was he fresh out of booze (at least in this room), but Lottie managed to chip through any self-confidence—false or not.

Retrieving the old photographs from his shirt pocket, he examined the portraits of the Grisé women. Maybe this was the perfect time to get out of town. Take a breather from *Lavier* or *Xottie* or *Xavottie*... There really wasn't a good way to combine those two names. Good thing they'd never be a celebrity power couple.

At any rate, a road trip was definitely in order. Besides, he'd heard Plantation Grisé was beautiful this time of year.

Actually, it was probably hot as fuck. The same as the rest of Louisiana. But since it seemed to be tied to the Villere household and he was going to write his fucking book after all, he needed to go.

Plus, it wasn't here. And that was as good a reason as any.

"Oh, honey, I am ever so sorry 'bout your poor daddy. To go in such a dreadful way! Well, we all know the bayou can be unforgiving, and Big Bubba sure don't discriminate. At least he died doin' something that made him happy. Your daddy sure loved to fish those waters."

Shock and disbelief trapped Nichole's face in a frozen, polite, and completely fake smile—the same smile she'd worn all evening while people expressed their condolences regarding her father's untimely death. Disappearance, really. They hadn't actually found a body.

But to have it so blatantly stated—this absurd theory that Daddy had been killed by an alligator? Who said that kind of thing?

Oh right, Miss Puts.

Eyes rimmed with concern and just a hint of smugness, pudgy hands folded over an even pudgier bosom, Miss Puts awaited her reply. Nichole knew what the older woman wanted. It's what a busy-body know-it-all like Miss Puts always wanted—praise for dipping her nose into business not remotely her own.

But Nichole was a good Southern girl with good Southern manners, so she simply said, "He did love to fish. Excuse me."

Swallowing against emotions threatening to bring fresh tears, she pushed her way through people crammed in the plantation manor's main receiving hall, that same plastic smile glued to her face. Brushing off expressions of concern, compliments of the beauty of Daddy's wake, and offers of food with polite—if not brusque—replies, her focus was on one thing and one thing only: the restroom door.

She could clearly see the edge of it tucked away in a black and white checkered hallway next to the kitchen entrance. With every step it seemed to move farther and farther away, like the distorted escape route in some horror movie, spinning and churning but never getting closer.

Nausea planted itself like a sprouting seed in her guts. Knotted roots erupted, sending vine-like tendrils throughout her body that promised to strangle her if she didn't reach the bathroom ASAP.

Stop it, Nic! Get ahold of yourself!

Blinking away tears, she choked down a few deep breaths in an attempt to relax. When she finally reached the restroom hallway, she was somehow able to open the door with forced calmness. Once inside, all bets were off. Shaking fingers managed to lock the antique latch before she collapsed onto the vanity.

Don't cry, don't cry, don't cry.

It took all of her resolve to not break down right there. Gathering every tattered shard of her emotions, she shoved them behind the invisible bubble that had protected her from the *others* since she was a little girl. She couldn't afford to lose control. She could never afford it. Control was the only safety net she had, and damned if she was going to let one stupid comment from Miss Puts shatter it.

A comment that wasn't even correct. As sure as she knew she was standing in the bathroom of the plantation house her father had worked at since she was born—a place she'd grown up and then spent every summer after her parents divorced—she knew Daddy hadn't been killed by a freaking alligator.

Once the tears were firmly at bay and her stomach no longer felt like it was turned inside out, she carefully inspected her reflection in the ornate mirror. Her puffy-eyed reflection stared back. Lack of sleep mixed with several nights of vodka tonics was definitely catching up—and it was the last thing she wanted. Damned if she was going to let Puts or anyone else catch her in a moment of weakness. She was successful. She was independent. And she was in control. Not looking the part, even for Daddy's wake, was *not* part of her plan.

And what was going on with her hair? The Louisiana humidity had already taken hold of her once sleek ponytail, forcing unwanted waves. Irritation replaced the nausea as she grabbed several bobby pins from her purse and twisted the brunette ends tightly together, securing them into a thick bun. Perhaps she was deliberately stalling, but going back out there meant enduring sympathy stares and expressions of pity from the dozens of people watching every move she made. Before she faced them again, she needed to make certain her wits, and her looks, were neat and tidy and back where they belonged.

She took another deep breath. She would get through this. She would smile, and endure their comments and condolences. And she would play along. She wouldn't argue—because experience taught her that never went well—even though she knew with every core of her being Daddy was not dead.

And before she went back to Baton Rouge, she'd find out what had happened to him.

CHAPTER TWO

"Now isn't that kitschy as fuck."

Stretching before him, live oaks curled over the long gravel drive at Plantation Grisé. Twisting bark and drooping Spanish moss, the trees framed a perfectly cliché plantation manor, complete with white columns.

"Any minute, Scarlett fucking O'Hara's going to come running down the drive," Julien muttered to himself. "*Fiddle-dee-dee. I'll never go hungry again!*"

He chuckled at his own impersonation and then chided himself for one, laughing at his own joke, and two, saying it out loud.

There was just something about driving *toward* a place known for enslaving one's ancestors that made a guy...tense. Not that all of his ancestors had been slaves—certainly few of the Villeres (which made Grandmere's connection to Plantation Grisé even stranger)—but he *was* a mixed bag of races.

The plantation was one of the oldest in Louisiana. Built in 1805 by Pascal Grisé, it was certainly around during Sanite and Laurent's lifetime. However, miles from New Orleans, it was hard to imagine how the Grisé family could have been affiliated with either Laurent or Sanite.

Although both Sanite and Laurent were known healers. So there was that. But nothing in Julien's research had even hinted of a Grisé connection. Nothing. Granted, the family history got a little sketchy the years following Laurent's death in 1816. What he had gathered only came from newspaper clippings and second-hand accounts.

The only thing apparent was that Sanite seemed to have lost her mind. Before Laurent's death she was a respected mistress of Voodoo—a woman people came to for healing potions of the body and mind. After, she was a feared queen whose sole purpose seemed to be revenge and hatred.

Grieving her brother's death was one thing. But to change so drastically because of one tragedy? It didn't make sense, and it certainly didn't explain the stories, arrests, and general fear from New Orleans citizens plaguing her until her mysterious disappearance and presumed death in 1821.

What happened to her was a mystery he'd like to solve not only for the book and for posterity, but for his own sanity. After becoming a pawn in her posthumous quest to avenge Laurent's death by punishing Lottie, he really wanted to understand the woman who used to inspire him but now filled his nights with nightmares.

Parking his rental car at the apex of the circle drive and base of the front staircase leading up to a broad expanse of front porch, he handed his keys off to a valet but shooed off the white gloved attendant that tried to take his bag.

"It's a backpack," he said. "I think I can manage."

The man looked put off by his statement. Most guests of this place probably loved being waited on, but it made Julien more than a little uncomfortable. Not only was it disconcerting to be served by a dark-skinned Creole at a plantation that once housed hundreds of slaves, but the man was wearing a white suitcoat. In suffocating heat. Beads of sweat coated the man's forehead and he was wearing a goddamn coat and gloves!

If the attendant wasn't enough to make Julien hate the place, the old people gathered in rocking chairs on the front porch and drinking iced tea (loaded with sugar, no doubt) sunk in the final nail. Too cliché, too stuffy, too country. It was a place for debutantes and polo, not his broke ass.

The inside of the plantation manor was worse. It was like an old lady exploded in the hallway. Gaudy, flowered, and a bad attempt to recreate Tara.

The attendant's desk was empty. A woman's voice drifted in from the room to his left. He stepped through a set of massive wooden doors and into an explosion of flowers and ribbons and fishing memorabilia.

"Jesus, who died in here?"

Two women busily packing up dishes stopped what they were doing to look at him. The older woman, a plump fifty-something matronly beast, looked pleasantly aghast, like she'd just heard a juicy piece of gossip that shocked and excited her at the same time. The other woman was beautiful and maybe twenty-six, with golden tanned skin and high cheekbones. Her full lips now pressed into a thin line as she narrowed her deep brown eyes and glared at him.

"My father," she said sharply.

Ah, shit.

"Um..." For some reason, the scowl on her face was making him fidget. "That sucks." *Sorry* would have been more appropriate. He shifted uncomfortably under the meager weight of his backpack.

"A little," the golden beauty replied with a smirk. Returning to the task of boxing up dishes, the scowl remained for only a few seconds longer before lines of fatigue and worry replaced it. She didn't look particularly sad, which seemed odd considering her father had apparently just died. But definitely weary, and wary.

"Hmm," he mumbled to himself.

"You here to check in?" Matronly Beast peered up at him from under the mass of artificial red curls sprayed into a stiff mass on her round head.

"Yeah."

"Nichole, sweetie, let me take care of this gentleman and then I'll help you finish up."

Nichole glanced his way, the scowl once again crossing her features for a brief second before it was wiped away. "Of course. Take your time." Her tone remained neutral, with almost a hint of pleasantness, but he could tell she was on edge. He was pretty sure that was his fault.

Well, it was a skill at least. Making beautiful women uneasy.

To think, he used to consider himself quite the charmer and dropper of women's panties. The Sanite/Lottie ordeal was really fucking with his head.

"Well, let's just get you all settled in, shall we?" The plump woman led him back out into the hallway where *Gone with the Wind* had purged and to the empty desk. "I'm Ruby Grisé," she said. "But you can call me Miss Puts. Everyone does. Guess 'cause I always *puts*," she snorted a little snicker, "everything and everyone in their place."

He was glad she was looking at the computer screen and not him. He was pretty sure she wouldn't care for what she saw. Pleasant would *not* describe his slightly aghast expression.

As Miss Puts clicked away at the keyboard, she rattled on about the plantation. Activities to do, when breakfast was served, the restaurant hours, quiet hours...

He only listened with half an ear. From the corner of his eye he could just make out Nichole wearily boxing up dishes. The emotions no longer hidden on her beautiful face now that she was alone, he could clearly see how exhausted and sad she really was. Every now and then, she'd stop the cleanup and close her eyes, her shoulders slumping like some huge elephant had climbed on them.

Man, him and his big mouth.

"And whatever you do," Puts whispered, leaning across the desk, "don't venture out into the swamp alone. There's a giant alligator out there, Big Bubba, that, well..." She gestured toward Nichole.

Whoa. What a fucked up way to die. No wonder Nichole was a mess. "You're kidding."

She shook her head. "'Fraid not."

He glanced at Nichole and the other woman did the same. "Mmm mmm," she murmured between pressed lips. "Poor dear." She shook her head, the artificial red stuff that kind of resembled hair not moving a millimeter. "Nichole!" she called, scampering (well...kind of waddling) from behind the desk and joining her in the other room. "Sugar, you look positively spent. Why don't you go get some rest? You can escort our guest to his room, number eight, on your way."

That was obviously the last thing Nichole wanted to do.

Miss Puts touched her arm. "Honey bear, I insist. I can finish this up. Or have Leroy do it."

More than likely, Leroy was the dark-skinned Creole who'd tried to take his backpack.

Nichole's sigh was visible, even from twenty feet away. "Okay. Sure. Thanks." She did actually look a little relieved. Until she looked in his direction.

Fuck. Well, whatever.

He planted the biggest, shit-eating grin on his face, and then did a flamboyant bow. Might as well go out with a bang and a smile...

She definitely rolled her eyes. She wasn't even subtle about it.

It just widened his grin.

She approached him with a new expression that was completely professional and devoid of any emotion. This girl was good at hiding, well, everything.

He liked it.

"I guess, follow me, Mr...?"

"Julien Villere. Or just Julien."

His name made her pause for a moment. It was brief, barely a flicker of hesitation, or recognition, or whatever it was, but he clearly saw it. Probably because he was so fascinated by her.

Turning, she strode for the front door and pulled it open. A gust of hot, humid wind smacked him in the face like a wet gym sock and loosened several strands of her sleek ponytail. She rushed to smooth them back in place, her hands quick and practiced.

Leading him down the steps and past the expansive wrap-around porch, she turned onto a brick pathway. He followed closely behind her. The smell of her perfume, something lavender based, mingled with the scent of freshly cut grass was entrancing.

Wind rustled through the oak trees lining the property in twisted rows, their century-old branches groaning in aching protest. It continually jostled her ponytail out of place, and she rapidly put it back together every time. The wind was so persistent, he wondered if she would eventually get tired of fixing her hair and turn it loose. He hoped so. He'd like to see that sleek black mane untamed.

He'd only known her twenty minutes, but he already knew there wasn't a chance in hell that would happen.

"For what it's worth," he said after a while of walking in silence. "I am sorry...about your father."

"Don't be. He ain't dead." Her face scrunched up in disgust. "Isn't," she corrected, her face scrunching again. "Never mind."

From the corner of his eye, he took in her profile as they walked. Her features were strongly Native

American, even more than Xavier's. But like himself and his brother, she was obviously a mix of many races.

And troubled. He could read it clearly in the furrow between her perfectly sculpted brows.

"That was his wake you were cleaning up back there, right?"

Her gaze stayed glued on the path before them. "Yes."

"But your father isn't dead?"

She remained fixated on the path as they covered half a dozen silent strides. Without warning, she stopped. Momentum carried him a few more steps before his brain could make the command to stop. He turned back to her.

Arms tightly crossed over her chest, her expression was both stern and pleading. "Forget I said anything, okay?"

Forgetting a dead man wasn't dead would be damn near impossible, but he agreed anyway. And then said, "If he isn't dead, where is he?"

"I don't know," she said, pushing past him. "And you said you'd forget it."

"Well, I won't run around discussing it with strangers if that's what you're worried about. But you've certainly piqued my curiosity."

"Un-pique it."

"Unlikely."

The dirtiest of looks flicked toward him from the corners of her eyes.

He tried to suppress it, but his grin fought back and a corner of his mouth lifted. "Okay, I'll try. No promises, though."

He was pretty sure she harrumphed.

No cracking that *one*, he thought.

They continued down the winding path for a few more silent minutes, through gardens of fragrant flowers and raised beds filled with a variety of plants, including sugar and cotton. The white mansion was a looming watchman behind them as the brick path turned into a mulch path. The live oaks became thicker the farther they walked from the manor, their branches dripping with Spanish moss swaying with every gusty breeze. He had a sneaking suspicion rain was on the menu in a matter of moments.

Luckily, rows of guesthouses quickly came into view. There were a little less than a dozen small, white wooden structures with expansive front porches nestled closely together. She stopped at the second to last in the row.

"Here's your room."

Surrounded by swamp on three sides, the structures were unmistakable in their original design.

"Converted slave quarters," he said. "How quaint."

"Is that a problem? They've been remodeled and are very nice."

"I'm sure they are. It's just a little...weird."

Her brows pushed together, more disdainful than confused. "Remodeling old slave quarters into B&Bs is pretty common. You're from New Orleans, how could you not know that?"

"How'd you know where I'm from?"

"I know Yat when I hear it."

"Fair enough." Yat, derived lovingly from "where y'at", was a very distinguishable, very NOLA accent.

"The bigger question is, you live in New Orleans and *this* bothers you?"

He felt his shoulders reach for his ears. "I mean, it just seems like such an odd thing to capitalize on."

"It's history. What *should* they do with the buildings?"

"I don't know." He gave her a purposeful once over. "I imagine we have a similar heritage. Don't you find it just a bit...unnerving?"

Her arms folded tightly over her chest. "No. Not at all. And I'm sure our heritage is nothing alike. *My* ancestors were slaves here. *I* was born here. And my daddy dedicated his entire life to this place. He loved this plantation. And if it was good enough for him, it should be good enough for you."

"I never said it wasn't good enough. I just said it was odd."

She harrumphed again and looked away.

"You still live here?" he wondered.

Her gaze stayed fixated on the distant bayou. "No. Baton Rouge."

"If you're so proud of your heritage here at Plantation Grisé, why'd you leave?"

Slowly, she turned back to him, dark eyes narrowed. With purposeful movements, her arms unfolded and her posture straightened. A gust of wind disturbed her sleek ponytail again, and with one fluid gesture she smoothed the strands along with her expression.

He raised his eyebrows.

"Enjoy your stay, Mr. Villere." Turning on her heel, she walked away. And right to the adjacent "guest room." Converted slave quarter number ten. He watched her until she disappeared into the cabin.

"Huh," he muttered with a shake of his head.

Glancing at the key in his hand, at the swamp surrounding him, and then back at the key, he turned for his cabin. Wasn't a whole lot of activity outside; he might as well unpack, have a cocktail, and check out the old slave quarter *remodeling*. Rumor said it was nice.

CHAPTER THREE

Daddy's scent still lingered heavily in the small, two-bedroom cottage. It was almost painful to breathe. Definitely bittersweet.

Every step an effort, Nichole trudged over to the couch and flopped on the worn, blue tweed fabric, sinking deeply into the lumpy cushions. She felt like she'd run a dozen marathons in the last forty-eight hours.

Exhausted didn't begin to describe her condition. Even her bones were tired. At least it explained why she'd run her mouth at that guy—what was his name?

Villere was the surname. She knew that. It was familiar though she wasn't sure why.

Not that it meant anything. There were plenty of common family names in Louisiana. His first name, though, that was different. J-something.

Right. Julien. Julien Villere.

What an arrogant prick. He had that cocky swagger most women drooled over, and looks to back it up—strong, square jaw, full lips, bright green eyes, and chiseled everything else. All details that obviously hadn't escaped him. And like some idiotic smitten teenager, she blurted to him what she'd managed to keep to herself since she arrived here. It just...came out. Oh well. What did she care about what he thought?

Plucking a throw pillow from the sofa corner, she hugged it tight. A picture of her with her father sat on the adjacent end table. She remembered the day that picture was taken very well. It was from six months ago—the last time she visited the plantation. She'd come down for the Mardi Gras celebration, surprising Daddy early in the morning. He'd been so happy to see her. They'd taken the picture on the bayou dock after an exceptional crawdad haul. Stacks of cages filled with hundreds of the crustaceans were lined up behind them and Daddy's eyes sparkled as much as the winter sun on the water. He'd always said he only needed two things in life: a good day on the bayou, and her, his baby girl.

God, she missed his smile. What she wouldn't do to have him back. To discover the truth behind his disappearance.

"What happened to you?" she whispered to the photo.

She might have only been back two days, but it was enough to know the police were clueless. Absolutely clueless. What they had was nothing but assumption.

And none of it made any sense.

An empty boat. That was pretty much it. So what if the boat was found abandoned, deep in the swamp, at Daddy's favorite fishing hole? So what if it happened to be in an area of the bayou where Big Bubba was frequently spotted? He hunted gators all the time and he knew those waters better than anyone. He was far too smart to let one stupid alligator take him down.

She felt the tears build in her eyes and hastily wiped them away. He wasn't dead, she reminded herself. She'd know if he were. She would have *felt* it. It's what she did. It's what she'd always done.

If she relaxed, she could feel *them* now, even if she couldn't see *them*. They were everywhere, surrounding her, stumbling around like confused children. But Daddy wasn't among *them*, so he couldn't be dead.

But where could he be?

They *might know.* They *see everything.*

She shuddered at the thought, quickly pushing it away.

Her internal voice was persistent, though. *Just let them in,* it said. *Everything you want to know is all around you.*

Clamping her jaw firmly shut, she shook her head at the empty room as she shoved *their* presence from her brain.

"No," she said to herself. As if saying the words aloud would quiet her inner voice. "There has to be another way."

She placed the pillow back delicately, as if doing so would preserve her father's lingering presence. If she wanted to get to the truth without letting *them* in, she had to think like a detective. Obviously, the police were missing something. Something huge. What had they seen at Daddy's fishing hole? Was there more evidence? Alligator tracks? Signs of a struggle? Anything besides an empty boat…?

She needed to see the site for herself. She knew him better than anyone. Surely there were clues...

That was it. She'd go to the dock, the one Daddy built deep in the bayou.

In the swamp. By herself.

Fear and panic rushed through her veins, turning her blood to ice. The idea alone made her want to run to her bedroom and dive under the covers.

But the other option was no less terrifying.

The window rattled as something hit it. Whipping her head toward the window, she screamed, her guts trying to leap out of her open mouth. Just the rain. Unfortunately, that little bit of knowledge didn't slow her heartbeat.

She needed to get a handle on her nerves. Control was her strength. She wasn't some silly little girl scared of her own shadow. Not anymore.

The soulless glass eyes of trophy animals from Daddy's many successful hunts all seemed to be staring at her, mocking and laughing. She didn't need their chastising stares. She was an expert at chastising herself.

Wait. Of course! He was an avid hunter. He had guns. Lots of guns. He wouldn't have gone out into the swamp without one, and neither would she. Big Bubba wasn't the only dangerous inhabitant of those murky waters.

Jumping up from the couch, she ran into his bedroom and headed straight for the closet. She pushed past his neatly hung shirts and slacks to where the gun cabinet stood against the back wall, safely out of sight.

It was locked, of course. He would never leave guns unsecured.

So where did he keep the key?

She spent the next thirty minutes searching drawers and boxes looking for the key. It was just as well. Outside, rain fell with ferocity. She wasn't going anywhere anytime soon.

Just as the rain began to taper, she found it. Tucked away in a cigar box and hidden under papers inside a desk drawer.

Rushing back to the closet, she unlocked the gun cabinet and reached inside. Her hand felt the cool metal of exactly what she was looking for. The corners of her mouth rose as she gently pulled out a 9mm and checked the magazine.

It was unloaded, of course. He kept the ammo locked in the cabinet as well—his one safety faux pas.

After popping a cartridge in the clip, she pulled out her waistband and tucked the gun securely against her back, quickly draping her shirt over the grip before heading toward the front door.

She glanced at her reflection in the mirror next to the door as she reached for the boat keys dangling from one of the hooks below. The frown lines were deep between her brows and she forced the muscles to relax, smoothing them away.

"Just act normal, Nichole," she said, taking a deep breath. "You can do this."

Fat droplets of water from the heavy oak limbs continued to splatter the ground even as the rain began to let up. Julien leaned back in his chair, a faux wicker number with a plush, floral seat cushion. He'd been sitting on this porch for a good hour, Jim Beam and Coke in one hand, the old photos of the Grisé sisters in the other, watching the rain drench the already saturated swamp and trying to determine his next steps.

First, he needed to find out exactly who the ladies Grandmere had built shrines for were. That was obvious. He'd start with Miss Puts. No doubt a place like this had a pretty good handle on the family history. Southerners were good like that anyway, and when you ran a business like this one, it definitely came with the territory.

The connection might be a tad more difficult to decipher. People in the 1800s didn't always document their slumming, so any interaction with the Villeres probably wouldn't have been declared.

He found his gaze flicking toward the cabin next door, the one occupied by that tough nut, Nichole, at regular intervals. Through the open window, he could see her milling about. Trying to be discreet, he would only sneak quick peeks, so he wasn't sure what she was doing, but she appeared to be looking for something. Actually, searching seemed like a better word.

The same as him.

When the final drops of rain finished falling from the clouds, she emerged from the cabin. She glanced his way, immediately tugging on the bottom of her blouse. He raised his glass in salute; her responding tight smile was obviously only out of politeness. As she hurried off the porch and down the mulch path heading toward the bayou, he couldn't help checking out her ass.

Nice, round, tight... And with a gun tucked into her shorts.

What the hell?

"Hey, Nichole!" he called, tossing his Beam and Coke on the end table and jumping from his seat. "Hey there, Speedy, hold up!"

She didn't slow as he jogged toward her and he didn't stop until he blocked her path. With a huge sigh, she halted her escape, folding her arms tightly against her chest and looking at him expectantly.

"Where you going in such a hurry?" he asked.

"How is that *possibly* any of your business?"

"Oh, I don't know. But it may have something to do with that gun you're hiding in your pants."

Her eyes widened briefly before narrowing. "I still don't see how that's any of your business."

"I've decided to make it my business," he said with a shrug. "So, where ya heading packin' that heat?"

With a roll of her eyes, she attempted to slip around him to the right, then left, and was blocked both times. The third time, she juked more aggressively, and unless he wanted to tackle her—which he kinda did—he was going to have to let her pass.

"You do realize I'm just going to follow you," he told her, inches from her heels.

"Please don't."

"Not going to happen. Unless you want to tell me why you need that gun."

"Why do you care?"

"I'm chivalrous like that."

"Give me a break." He couldn't see her face, but he could definitely *hear* the eye-roll.

"No, really. I mean, opening doors, carrying heavy packages, not letting girls run off alone to the swamp carrying a gun... Wait. That's where you're headed, isn't it? Rumor has it your father was killed by an alligator, right? And you don't think he's dead, so you're going to look for him, aren't you?"

She remained silent.

"The gun is for protection. Okay, I get it. Smart."

"Well, I'm glad that's settled," she said over her shoulder. "You can quit following me now."

"No. I'm still going with you. No man of chivalry would allow a lady to face a man-eating alligator alone."

"Do you really think I'm going to let you come with me?"

"Yes. I'm persistent."

"I can say no."

"You can. It probably won't help."

They arrived at a rickety wooden dock extending into still, murky waters. A flat- bottom boat tied to a pier was eerily motionless, like a ghost vessel with its stillness. "Little Nicky" was written in scrolling cursive across the front.

"Your father's boat," Julien observed.

It was the first time she looked his direction that her expression wasn't filled with irritation. "Yes," she said simply.

He nodded solemnly. "Then you must understand why I can't, in any good conscience, let you get on that boat alone."

Her chest rose and fell in a silent sigh. "Fine. Get in."

He felt like an eight-year-old boy who just discovered he was finally getting a puppy. After stepping carefully into the small boat, he immediately went to the controls and began getting a feel for it. Simple enough—steering wheel, key, no gas pedal, but there was a throttle...

"What are you doing?"

Nichole stood beside him, arms once again crossed tightly over her chest, pressing her breasts together so that the crests spilled over the top of her shirt. Lavender bliss floated over from her, tying his tongue for a second.

"Um... Driving?"

"Have you ever operated a boat before?"

"No, but—"

She actually pushed him aside. "Go sit down," she said, tossing a life jacket at him. "And try not to fall into the water."

It definitely was not *her* first time at the helm, and within minutes they had pulled away from the dock and were sliding smoothly through the water.

CHAPTER FOUR

What started as an open pool of water turned into a twisting maze of vegetation. Julien was pretty sure there was a channel hidden among the shadows and roots, but he couldn't begin to tell where. Luckily, Nichole navigated with ease, like she'd traveled these waters a million times.

Still, she seemed nervous.

Eyes darting back and forth, she scanned the thick vegetation and even thicker shadows constantly, even as she steered the boat around roots and fallen logs.

It was understandable. After all, a man-eating alligator roamed these waters. One that had supposedly killed her father.

Except strangely enough, she wasn't looking down. Her focus was out among the trees, not in the water around the boat. Last time he checked, alligators didn't walk upright.

Did she think her father was just wandering around?

Well, questions weren't answered if they weren't asked.

"What are you looking for?"

She glanced at him in surprise. "Oh, nothing," she said with a shake of her head.

"My ass."

She ignored him. After his inquiry, her gaze stayed more focused on the water and the area in front of the boat. Her attention still flickered about now and again, but she seemed to be trying to be subtle about it.

He had no idea what to make of it. Normally, he'd just press until he had the answers he wanted, but she seemed pretty good at evading his questions, so he decided to simply observe. For now.

It didn't get him far. She knew her way around the swamp, yes. She was completely frightened by the swamp, yes. Did that fear have to do with her father's disappearance? He had no idea.

After twenty minutes or so, they arrived at a stand-alone dock nestled among a forest of cypress trees. Nichole idled up to it and then killed the engine, straddling both boat and dock until their vessel eased to a stop. After tying it off, she stepped onto the wooden platform hovering inches above the murky waters.

Besides Nichole, the dock also housed a ratty camp chair and some fishing equipment sitting below a rudimentary, tin-roof shelter.

"Daddy's favorite fishing spot," she explained as he joined her on the dock. "It's where he disappeared. Or where they found the boat."

Julien glanced around the structure. "And supposedly eaten by alligator?"

"Yeah..." Her voice was distant, thoughtful. He hoped he hadn't upset her, but she didn't seem upset, per se. More...pensive.

"But there isn't any evidence of alligator attack," he noted. "No blood, or you know, anything else."

"I see that."

"So what warranted the 'death by alligator' allegation?"

Her focus still scanning the dock, water, and trees around them, she shrugged. "They found his boat here. Empty."

"That's it? Hardly enough evidence."

For the first time since he'd met her, she offered him a sincere smile. It was sarcastic, but sincerely sarcastic. And he'd gladly take it.

"It's a small town," she said. "People tend to jump to conclusions."

"That's one hell of a leap. No body, empty boat, and they have a funeral. No wonder you don't think he's dead."

"It's more than that, but yeah." She scanned the dock again.

"Oh? Like what?"

Ignoring his question, she continued to investigate. She examined the fishing pole, a hunk of shriveled up bait still attached, then peered into the cooler and looked under the chair and in the cup holder.

"Was he a drinker? Could he be on a bender? In my drug days, I could have easily disappeared for a week on a bender. My family probably would have loved to throw my funeral. Probably would have gladly put me in a coffin too," he added with a chuckle.

She gave him a WTF look.

"I was a bit of a shit," he explained. "Still am."

The quick bob of her eyebrows said she agreed. "No, he wouldn't be on a bender. Daddy isn't *that* kind of drinker. And he's never missed a day of work in his life."

"Admirable," Julien muttered.

Daddy definitely sat on a pedestal in Nichole's world. It wasn't something he could relate to, that was for sure. Maybe when he was twelve and naïve.

For a place filled with insects and wildlife, without the buzz of the boat engine, the swamp seemed incredibly quiet. Nothing moved, not even the water. So still it was a perfect mirror, the reflection of the cypress trees crisply clear. The layer of moss clinging to the water surface looked like it hadn't moved in decades.

Which is why the movement caught his eye in the first place. Normally, he wouldn't have noticed it, but in this lifeless swamp, even a buzzing fly would have been like a stampeding elephant.

Nichole was still pondering her father's fishing setup when he moved to get a better look. Squinting, he strained his eyes to try and differentiate between shadow, tree, and water. It wasn't easy, and for a moment he was certain he'd been mistaken. But then he saw it again. There was definitely something out there.

And it was big. As tall as a man, but didn't resemble anything human, at least not the way it moved. It was too far away and the light too dim to make out any features. But its movements were halting, almost lumbering, lurching. Like a heavy piece of trash caught in an inconsistent wind. He studied it a few minutes before finally turning to Nichole.

"What is that?" he asked, pointing.

Her gaze jerked up and toward his outstretched finger. Her eyes narrowed and then widened, jumping upward toward the sky before she practically launched herself into the boat. "C'mon, let's go!"

"So you saw it?"

She shook her head frantically. "There's nothing there, but the sun is setting. We need to get out of the swamp before dark."

He glanced first toward the location of the mystery object, or animal, or whatever it was. Sure enough, it was gone. He looked upward and then glanced at his watch. "It's like, six o'clock. We still have a couple hours—"

"There's no time. Get in the boat, Julien, or swim back!"

As scared as she looked, he had no doubts she'd leave him. Hell, he was surprised she hadn't already left.

The motor sputtered to life as he clambered in. He barely had both feet inside before she'd untied the boat and they were speeding away from the dock.

It didn't matter how well she knew this bayou, he was sure they were traveling way too fast to be safe. And judging by the panicked expression on her exotic features, he was also sure she couldn't be convinced to slow down.

To avoid looking at all the obstacles and near-miss crashes, he kept his gaze firmly planted on the trees as they whizzed by, just as his grip stayed firmly attached to the side of the boat.

What had her so scared? It had to be whatever he saw in the distance, right? Maybe it was some sort of animal, one that only came out at dusk.

He had lived his entire life in New Orleans. He was a city boy through and through. His knowledge of the city and its history was vast. This backwoods shit? No clue.

Through the blur of trees, he suddenly caught a flash of milky white eyes attached to a withered old man. Simply standing waist deep in the water, next to a tree.

"What the—?"

"Don't look, don't look, don't look!" Nichole murmured frantically.

"What? Why?" He twisted in his seat. The old man was still there, standing motionless, and quickly disappearing into the distance. "Who is that?"

She patted her back, checking that the gun was still in her waistband.

"Um, Nichole..."

The boat picked up speed. If it moved any faster, Julien was sure they could fly if he stuck his arms out like wings.

"Nichole, baby, I am pretty fond of living..."

"It's fine."

He was pretty sure it wasn't. Luckily it was only minutes later that they emerged from the trees and into the open water. She barely slowed when they pulled up to the dock, the boat slamming into the bumpers with a thud. Killing the engine and jumping out in one fluid motion, she haphazardly tied off the boat before hastening up the walkway.

"Um..." He remained in the boat as it bobbed up and down in its own wake, watching Nichole's back as she scurried away. "Okay. I'm cool. Pretty sure I can find my way back, thanks."

He glanced around. There may have been a weird old man in the swamp, but there was nothing here. Well, besides cicadas and whatever else chirped in the trees.

The sun slipped behind the trees, making the murky waters look even darker, inky even. That was his cue to get the hell out of there. He might not be as freaked out as poor Nichole, but he was definitely feeling the creep factor. Maybe he should be concerned there was an old blind man standing alone in alligator infested waters, but at this point he wasn't sure what to think other than he'd found himself in a weird, fucked up situation.

And to be honest, he was more concerned about what was going on with Nichole and her missing father than some crazy old swamp dude. In fact, if he hoped to catch her, he needed to get on it. She was booking it and so would he.

The planation manor darted in and out of the thick trees as her feet pounded quickly against packed earth. The worn pathway was as familiar to her as her own face, but one she normally avoided. She actually tried to avoid *anything* leading to the swamp if she could. Had she really seen what she thought she had? Had Julien?

The swamp frightened her for more than one reason. *They* seemed stronger in the tree-filled bayou. Like the shadows in the water gave *them* power. On fishing trips with her father, when they ventured off the main channel, *their* presence was thick. Penetrating. Smothering. Even now, she could feel *them* all around her and she was having a hard time blocking them.

It was like they'd followed her out of the swamp. She felt like she had a blinking "blue-light special" circling her head.

"Nichole! Wait."

Her gaze swiveled over her shoulder to see Julien coming toward her in a dead run. The roaring of blood in her ears kept her from hearing anything else he was shouting. God, he was the last thing she needed right now. And why was he being so damn nosy? Chivalry was one thing, but insisting that he go along with her...well, that was pushing it.

Thankfully, she was just far enough ahead to lose him. The hidden shortcut to the cottages was just off the main path. A thick line of tall bushes revealed the small path she was looking for. She stopped for a millisecond to cup the sides of the branches and pull back just enough space to allow her to leap through.

A tinge of guilt slowed her momentum when she heard her name again. The concern in his voice tugged at her conscience, but she couldn't let him catch up—she needed to think, needed to get a handle on the tumultuous emotions churning through her body.

The many twists and turns through the trees and bushes made her virtually disappear, and that's exactly what she wanted. She wished everything stopping her from finding the truth about her father would disappear.

She glanced back one final time. There was no sign of him. It worked, at least for the time being. She would deal with him later.

Relief flushed her face as the back porch of her cottage came into view.

Stopping at the threshold, she panned left then right just to make sure. She was definitely alone. Heart racing, she swiped the stinging sweat from her eyes before pushing the door open. Times like these she was glad people rarely locked their doors out here in the boondocks.

The wall of icy, air-conditioned air was a welcome relief as it instantly seemed to suck the heat from her body. Carefully shutting, and then locking, the door behind her, she made her way to the kitchen counter.

Adrenaline coursing her veins made her hand shake when she gripped the handle of the gun still tucked in her waistband. As gently as she could muster, she pulled it out and placed it on the counter before filling a glass with water.

She was halfway through it when movement from the front window caught her eye. Julien was walking at a fast pace directly toward the cottage.

Shit.

Slipping into the nearest bedroom, she ducked behind the wall hiding her from the front window view. Heavy footsteps sounded on the front porch and then a loud knock at the door. "Nichole, girl. You in there?"

She cringed. He sounded even more concerned than he had in the woods. Should she…?

She took a step forward and then stopped. Facing him now would be a mistake. Even if she was being awful making him worry, she needed to pull it together before she apologized for abandoning him at the dock. Not only because she was a wreck of frazzled nerves, but she needed to decide what to say about what they saw out there.

His footsteps led him off the porch and she carefully peered around the corner. She couldn't quite see where he was, so she leaned deeper into the living room until she could see his back through the window. He just stood there, staring down toward the swamp.

What was he…?

He suddenly turned back around. With a startled scream she somehow managed to muffle, she jumped back into the other room. Sure he'd spotted her, she held her breath and waited for the knock.

That never came.

After a few agonizing minutes of hiding, guilt gnawing at her emotions, she decided to dust off her big girl pants and face him like the grown up she was supposed to be. She'd simply let him know she was okay, apologize for running off, and then offer to explain everything later if he asked, which she was positive he would.

But he was no longer standing out front. She made her way to the porch and caught a glimpse of his wide back as he headed for the manor.

Guilt devoured her. He seemed genuinely concerned, which was baffling since he barely knew her. It was obvious he found her attractive, but that didn't explain anything. Guys like him wanted to sleep with her. They didn't worry over her problems.

Even if she couldn't deny she found him kinda, sorta—a lot—attractive, it didn't matter. This wasn't remotely the time. So she brushed it, and his concern, away. One thing was for sure, she'd have to be more careful around him. He'd already seen and she'd already blurted too much.

At the moment, though, she had other things to fret about. Like how was she going to find out what happened to her father?

The fishing dock left just as many questions as answers. No sign of a struggle, no blood, a half-empty beer… It was like Daddy had just vanished into thick, muggy, Louisiana air.

So now what?

With a sigh, she glanced around the room. It hadn't changed in years. Still the same white poster bed with lilac printed bedspread, crisply made of course, same French country vanity with photos lining the mirror, hair products neatly arranged on one side, makeup on the other. It was a reminder that no matter how much she'd changed since leaving the plantation, she was always the same.

And so were her problems.

It was so much harder to escape *them* here. And without Daddy's strong support, it was an exhausting task.

Maybe she should just give in. Maybe she had to.

With a grimace, Nichole delicately sat on the bed to avoid ruffling the bedspread. She was going to have to do it. Since going to the dock hadn't yielded any answers, she was going to have to ask for *their* help.

It would be a few hours before she could even attempt it. Not only did their strength increase when the sun vacated the sky, but she needed to mentally prepare herself. That alone could take all night.

CHAPTER FIVE

"Okay. That's weird."

Nichole had just disappeared. One second he was chasing after her, glimpses of her pink blouse flashing in and out of the trees. The next? Nothing.

He slowed to a stop and scanned the forest around him. There was only one damn path, where could she have gone?

"Jesus," he muttered, rubbing his hand over his scalp.

The last fucking thing he needed, the last fucking thing he wanted, was to be caught up in some paranormal hoopla. He should just walk away. Find out what he needed for his research and then bail.

That was what he should do... Instead, he called Nichole's name again.

Only crickets and cicadas and the annoying buzz of mosquitos answered. He smacked one of the little bloodsuckers away.

"Nichole!" he called again.

Another bloodsucker latched onto his neck. The slap of hand against flesh stung almost as much as the bite.

Okay, she obviously wasn't around. Maybe she was simply faster than he thought. She might be back at the cabin. And he was getting eaten alive.

At a brisk pace, he hurried up the path, covering the last thousand feet in a few measly seconds. He stopped at Nichole's cabin first, knocking firmly on the door. Once more he called her name, and once again he was met with silence.

Fuck. Now he was really worried. Stepping off the porch, he looked down the path leading to the bayou. Creepy old dudes in the swamp, strange indistinguishable man/animal/werewolves lumbering around, man-eating alligators, people disappearing, and now this. He should go back and look for her. Maybe she was hurt, or worse.

He glanced toward the cottage and caught a flurry of movement.

That little—

She was inside all along.

Fine. He knew when to step back.

Pivoting on his heel, he turned away, walking past his cabin for the manor. He couldn't remember everything that old bag Miss Puts said when he arrived, but he distinctly recalled a bar and a restaurant. Food and alcohol (mostly alcohol) were definitely in order. Maybe Puts would even be up there and he could actually accomplish something instead of chasing after some girl who obviously couldn't give two shits about him.

The pictures of the Grisé sisters were still tucked in his pocket. Time to find out who they were and how they related to his family.

Unfortunately, the old lady wasn't at the big house, the help explaining she left at six but would be back in the morning. Bright and early. Not that Julien did bright, or early.

The mission wasn't all lost. There was a big, empty bar—save for the bartender, a young, dark-skinned man with short-cropped hair and a bright white, over-bleached smile that outshone his crisp white suit coat and gloves.

What was it with the gloves at this place?

The bartender wiped the wooden bar with a soft rag as Julien took a seat. "What can I do for ya, sir?"

"A Sazerac and a menu."

"Yessir." He handed over a menu printed on paper meant to look old.

"And lose the 'sir' nonsense," Julien added as he took the menu.

"I don't know that I can do that, sir."

"Seriously. It's making me uncomfortable. Between staying in old slave quarters, and being waited on hand and foot by—" He shook his head. "Look, I won't tell your boss. We're the only ones in here..."

The other man looked around the room, peering over each of Julien's shoulders and then behind him, like someone might be hiding among the liquor bottles. "You sure?"

"Of course. Jesus, what do I look like?"

The bartender exhaled in an explosive sigh. "Man, you have no idea how exhausting that is." His entire accent, tone of voice, posture, everything, changed.

Julien grinned. "I bet. What's your name?"

"Shay."

He took Julien's outstretched hand and shook it firmly as Julien completed the introduction.

"So what brings you out here?" Shay asked as he selected bitters from the row of paper covered bottles lining the back of the bar top like a picket fence. "You're not exactly our normal clientele."

"No shit." Julien shook his head again as he skimmed the menu. Every other *guest* he'd seen was twenty years his senior and several shades lighter. And he was pretty damn fair given his heritage. "I'm here for research."

"Oh yeah?" Shay paused the cocktail mixing. "Bourbon or rye?"

"Bourbon."

"What kind of research?" the younger man asked as he retrieved the bottle of liquor.

"The family type. Say, how much do you know about this place?"

"Just what they print in the brochure."

That didn't surprise him. The man couldn't be more than twenty-three. "I take it you aren't from here."

"Naw, man. Houma. I've been here a year though." Shay presented the cocktail.

It looked like he would have to wait until morning after all. He took a sip. "Delicious."

Shay smiled proudly.

Attention turned to the menu, Julien's stomach grumbled in anticipation. Typical southern fare: po' boys, Étouffée, red beans and rice, numerous fried dishes. "What do you recommend?"

"It's all pretty good. The alligator is especially tasty."

He had been prepared to order the red fish, but Shay's recommendation turned his thoughts to Nichole and her missing father, and he decided some fried reptile sounded pretty damn good after all.

He put the order in and picked up his cocktail, leaning back in the high back leather bar stool. He finished the drink in one smooth swallow, sighing when the aroma wafted up from the glass, the distinctive smell of bourbon and licorice drowning out the pungent smell of the furniture polish coating the wooden bar.

The glass hit the bar with a thud. "I'll take another."

Shay laughed. "You sure you don't just want a shot?"

"Okay. Give me a Sazerac with a shot of bourbon back."

"That bad of a day?"

Shay handed over the shot first and Julien gratefully slammed it.

"You have no idea. Between the girl and the swamp..."

Shay visibly shuddered at the mention of "swamp."

Julien felt his eyes narrow. He blinked it away. "I take it you don't like the swamp?" he noted nonchalantly.

"That place seriously freaks me out. Stay away from it. "

Interest officially piqued. "Why is that?"

"Well, besides the man-eating alligators, there are fuc—" He abruptly straightened up, like doing so would put the parking brake on the foul language. The brainwashing went deep with this one.

Shay leaned forward, once again looking in every corner of the bar for spies. "They don't like us talking about this with guests, but there are dead people out there."

Okay, not what he was expecting. "Like corpses?"

Shay nodded. "Ones that walk."

"So, zombies?"

"Exactly. They don't try to eat you or anything, but they're still freaky as shit."

"I can imagine." He thought back to the old man standing vacant-eyed and knee-deep in water and could only imagine that's what Shay referred to. That man might have been crazy, or homeless, but he hadn't appeared to be dead. At least not from the quick glance Julien had gotten. "Have you seen them?"

"No, man. I don't go near that shit."

The foul language curb-check had obviously gone out the window.

"Warning heeded." And mentally filed away for future investigation.

The alligator was far more satisfying than he expected. Even though Nichole wasn't convinced her father—a man he had never even met—had been dinner for one of the prehistoric beasts, every deep fried and breaded bite was filled with the rich taste of revenge.

Three more cocktails and a couple shots later, Julien stumbled out of the manor and down the dark path toward the cabins. Even though solar-powered lanterns lined the edges on both sides, they barely put out enough light to cast a few shadows on the brick. The moon couldn't be counted on either, ducking in and out of the clouds. Mostly in.

Once the brick turned to mulch, the path got even darker. The trees thickened, live oak branches twisting overhead, blocking even more of the feeble moonlight. It was strange how much darker it was here than New Orleans. He got that this wasn't the city, but he'd been in the country before and it wasn't *this* dark. It was like every drop of light was sucked into the earth.

There was a light in Nichole's window, though. Like a beacon, it called to him, luring him to her porch steps. Even though his brain was a little bourbon foggy, he quickly remembered their earlier escapade, where she'd ditched him in the bayou and then hid in her house. That light wasn't a beacon, it was a damn lighthouse, warning him from certain death among rocky shores.

A warm breeze drifted up from the swamp, bringing with it the sickly sweet smell of decay. At first, he thought nothing of it, wrinkling his nose and heading for his own cabin. But when the scent hit him a second time, stronger and more pungent, he paused. Shay said there were dead people walking the swamp. Julien may have even seen one (or more likely a crazy old man). Maybe he should investigate. It could add a little flavor to his book in progress...

He didn't even want to think it could be Nichole's father. He wasn't going to think it. A fat, bloated raccoon was more likely.

Pulling one of solar lanterns from the soil where it was doing a piss-poor job of providing light, he made his way toward the smell. Not surprisingly, it got stronger as he neared the water. Thankfully his senses were bourbon dulled, or it would probably be overwhelming.

As he approached the water's edge and the small wooden pier with Nichole's father's boat attached, the smell became so strong, he had to cover his nose with the neck of his T-shirt.

"That better be one giant raccoon," he muttered into the fabric.

The moon had ducked behind the clouds again, and the useless lantern was pretty much just casting murky shadows a full two inches in all directions. He stopped a good ten feet from the water. He might be curious, but he wasn't stupid.

Besides the overwhelming smell of death, there wasn't a lot going on. Once again, the bayou seemed incredibly quiet. No mosquitos, no crickets, no frogs, nothing. It was like the sound had joined the light and taken a vacation.

Snapping branches from somewhere behind him shattered the silence. With a jump, he turned, pointing the lantern toward the source. He might as well try to shoot laser beams out of his eyes. All he saw was a little black, and maybe some more black.

It was probably just that raccoon's friends anyway.

The moon broke through the clouds right when he turned back to the water. Narrowing his eyes, he leaned forward.

"What the hell?"

Hundreds of floating shapes dotted the cove, silver bumps rising out of the normally flat surface of water. He took one step forward and then stopped mid-stride. Fish. Dead fish, but still just fish.

Was that what stunk so badly? They weren't here earlier. Would they already be rotten enough to stink up the entire state of Louisiana? Even worse than Bourbon Street?

Apparently.

It *was* hot as balls out here; shit probably started rotting before it even died.

Scanning the water one final time, he shuddered. Moonlight, weak as it was, danced off the slimy corpses. Hundreds might have been a low estimate. There looked to be thousands. He had no idea what could have killed them, but the scene was nothing short of disgusting.

Well, mystery solved. Definitely not zombies, but still creepy as shit.

His pace back up the path was one gear down from a jog. He made it fifty feet before the stench hit him like a sack of bricks, bypassing his shirt shield and searing his lungs.

"Ugh." He had to fight the gag reflex.

Just to his left, maybe five feet from where he walked, branches snapped again, sending a shiver of adrenaline straight to his heart. He didn't even look this time, not that it would have made a difference.

His solar lamp was now putting off less light than a lightning bug.

Time to get the fuck out of Dodge. Raccoon or no raccoon, between the fish corpses, the eerily quiet swamp, and the reek of death all around him, he was officially freaked out.

Skipping jog gear, he broke into dead run gear, declining to breathe until the light in Nichole's window greeted him. Jagged rocks or no jagged rocks, he was damn happy to see it.

It was possible he was the biggest pansy around, but he didn't stop running until he reached his front porch. Tossing the useless lantern aside, he doubled over, clasping his knees as thick, humid air rushed in and out of his lungs.

In between gasps, he couldn't help but laugh at the ridiculousness. Jesus, dead fish? Who woulda fucking guessed?

Well, that definitely warranted a nightcap before bed. Luckily, he kept a bottle of Beam handy, in addition to the flask he almost always had in his pocket. One (or two) more drinks oughta do it.

Tomorrow, he'd corner old Miss Puts and get some answers. Then he could get the hell away from this place and back to New Orleans where stenches came from sewers and dead bodies were slightly less common. It wouldn't be soon enough.

The light in Nichole's window caught his eye and filled him with a little regret. What about her? He'd love to help her figure out what happened to her father.

Actually, he'd love to do a lot of things, but obviously that wasn't a ship she wanted to sail. So he would get his answers and get out. End of story.

CHAPTER SIX

"The light of a flame is their beacon," Gran's voice echoed in her head. *"Be careful, baby, 'cause they'll come floodin' back. It's what they'll look for."*

Lit match inches from the candle wick, Nichole paused. She knew what came next. Knew she had to do this if she wanted answers.

But damn if it didn't scare the holy hell out of her. Refusing to move but too afraid to light the candle, her hand hovered in mid-air, flickering flame quickly devouring the match.

Her body trembled as a shiver swept down her spine. This was her only option and she couldn't let fear hold her back. Another day of not knowing what happened to Daddy was breaking her to her core.

An hour ago, she had come close to calling her mama in Baton Rouge— that's how desperate and rattled she was. Just to hear a familiar voice, just to be able to tell someone, anyone, what she was about to attempt was so...tempting. She stopped before hitting the send button. Nothing good would have come out of that conversation.

Her relationship with her mother had always been strained, and it got worse after her parents divorced. Nichole's abilities (she refused to call them a gift) came from Daddy's side of the family. Not only did her mama not understand the problems she faced every day of her life, she had grown to resent them and the inherent bond Nichole shared with Daddy, and especially Gran, because of them. Bringing it up only led to bitterness and eye rolls.

If only Gran were still alive. She'd know what to do—she had the ability too. Of course, she wouldn't approve. She'd always steered Nichole away from it. Said it was too much for a young girl to deal with. But that was no longer the case. Nichole was a grown woman now, more than capable of taking care of herself.

Unfortunately, excelling at a career and being able to pay the bills wouldn't do a damn thing for her now. She might as well still be that scared little girl hiding under blankets, hoping and praying the ghosts wouldn't find her.

Sharp pain flicked her fingertips as the flame reached the end of the match and singed her flesh. Shaking it until it went out, she tossed the curled, blackened wood next to the unlit candle and shoved to her feet.

The dresser mirror revealed the beginnings of blotchy pink hives on her neck and chest. Mentally prepping for this moment had backfired. She was even more stressed about it. She sure could work herself up.

"You need to chill out," she whispered to herself.

A drink would help her nerves.

It was a horrible idea. Making herself more vulnerable would only give *them* more control, more access to her thoughts and what scared her. But she needed some way to relax.

She grabbed a glass from the drying rack next to the sink and then reached into the cabinet above her head. One drink. That's all she'd have. One couldn't hurt, could it?

Scooting a kitchen chair back, she sat with a heavy sigh, plopping the nearly full bottle of whiskey next to her glass on the table. The brown liquor swayed back and forth hypnotically, the promise of relaxation echoing with every wave. She poured a carefully measured shot, took a sip, said a mental, "what the hell," and finished the liquor off.

What a day. What an exhausting, mentally draining, emotionally shattering day. From cleaning up the wake (that alone would have warranted a shot), to her harried journey into the swamp carrying a gun of all things, to seeing—she refused to even give it a name—to her frantic race to get away from Julien... It was like a *Choose Your Own Adventure* gone wrong.

God, Julien. She wasn't sure what to think about him. He seemed to have this uncanny insight into her mind. And like an idiot, she'd blurted something she shouldn't. Even worse, he'd seen...*it*.

So not only did he know too much, but he was obviously watching her. And she didn't like it. Not one bit. Anger might make her pissed at the situation, but guilt kept her from telling him off. No matter how she felt about his intrusion into her personal life, she'd completely abandoned him. She'd left him stranded in a potentially dangerous situation while she ran off like a frightened child. When really, cockiness aside, he'd been nothing but a gentleman. And seemed truly sympathetic to her situation.

God, she hated feeling confused. Hated not being in control of her emotions, the whole situation... Why was he so damn curious anyway, and why did he even care? Hell, why did *she* care about offending *him*?

She poured another shot and drank it in one swallow. Her face crinkled at the fumes and her breath felt like it was on fire.

The glass landed on the table with a thud. Okay, that was it. She needed to get to it while the liquid courage burned through her veins.

The bedroom might have only been steps away, but it seemed to take fifteen minutes to get there. She paused in the doorway, her feet suddenly encased in concrete. The dark candle taunted her, chiding her for her unfinished task.

Inhaling deeply, she tried to relax the vice grip squeezing her heart.

"C'mon, Nichole. You can do this."

It took muscles she didn't know existed, but somehow she was able to drag her feet to the candle, and then even more miraculously, slowly sink onto the cool wooden floor.

Reaching for her cell phone, she laid it next to the candle with her mama's number cued up—just in case.

"Here goes nothin'."

With hands shaking like an alcoholic withdrawing from a weekend bender, she lit the candle. The flame flickered a golden hue that danced along the walls in the otherwise dark room.

She squeezed her lids tightly and bowed her head. Hands tightly bound in her lap, her lips moved in silent prayer for God's protection. She hoped it would be enough.

Her hands were so clammy from sweat they felt like she'd dipped her palms in water, and her heart pounded so strongly she was sure it was visible through her shirt.

She seriously needed to calm down. Drawing in a full breath, she intentionally held it for a few seconds before slowly blowing it out through her nose. It took a minute, but with conscious effort and slow steady breathing, her body and mind began to relax.

Just as Gran taught her, she imagined a door to the wall separating her from death. Once the image appeared—an old wooden door with peeling black paint—the next step was to envision it opening.

Her heart raced back to a gallop. It went against everything she'd been taught to protect herself. Since the age of eleven, her abilities were under strict lock and key. There was no breaking them. At least that's what she always thought, and hoped. She didn't know exactly what waited for her on the other side, but it was guaranteed to be bad.

"You can do this, Nichole," she whispered to herself. "You have to."

When the door cracked open, she instantly felt *them*. A certain overcharged readiness suggested that many of them were growing extremely impatient. And they were angry. Very angry. She could hear their thoughts berating and accusing her for delaying communication all this time. An unsettling rumble through the room nauseated her as they filled the air with a thundercloud of disapproval.

And God, there were so many of them. Like a gathering army lining up, coming at her in full force. Hungry tigers ready to pounce on their prey.

Feelings of dread slammed into her thoughts and her eyes flashed open.

Oh God!

The room was filled with corpses.

Horrific decaying faces and twisted, rotten bodies surrounded her, reaching for her, crowding her, touching her, whispering her name.

She screamed. "No, no, no, no!! Get back!! It's too much! Stop!!"

Clamping her eyes shut, she mentally slammed the conjured door.

Body trembling, breathing so rushed it bordered on hyperventilating, she sat completely motionless, trying desperately to get air to the bottom of her lungs.

She could feel them pushing against the door, and if she wanted it to stay closed she needed to calm the panic—a panic that continued pulsing through her body and mind despite her best efforts.

What just happened? According to everything Gran had taught her, she should have been able to contact them while keeping them out of her head. But she could still feel their anger and desperation, their life regrets, their loneliness as deeply as if the emotions were her own.

With a few shuddering deep breaths, she was able to lock the mental door. It was such a simple idea, the door, but if she concentrated hard enough, it always worked. Just as it did now.

Slowly, the earthbound ghosts' presence eased from her mind. As always, she could still sense them just beyond the peeling black door, but unlike the bombardment that had just flooded her, it was a mere tickle at the base of her skull.

Another deep breath, this one smooth and without hiccups, and she slowly cracked open her eyes with a whisper, "Please let them be gone."

Rage floated through the air like thick tendrils of toxic smoke. It twisted around in colors of red and purple and black. Covering his nose with his shirt, he ran through the room trying to find an escape, batting at the hate and trying to clear a path in the air that was safe to breathe.

It choked his lungs anyway. Filling them with such putrid emotions he wanted to retch. The room went nowhere. Everywhere he turned he hit a wall. No doors. No windows. No escape.

Panicked and starving for oxygen, he sucked in a deep breath. The poison immediately saturated his blood, ripping through his body with shrapnel that shredded his veins.

They ended at his brain. Screaming, he grabbed his head in pain and fell to his knees. Every emotion filled him. Not just hate, but love, and despair, and loss, and overwhelming loneliness.

His babies. He just wanted his babies back.

But Julien didn't have any children. He'd never even had a scare. Still, he could feel their absence as strongly as if they'd been ripped from his nonexistent womb.

Flashes of memories shot through his brain. A white man of about forty, dressed in fine, 19th century clothing, a smile on his handsome face as he held out his hand in invitation. Lust, then love, then anger and betrayal, ending finally with hatred so thick it was like syrup, flooded his body all at once.

Laurent Villere, shot and lying dead in the street. Grief so strong he could barely think, barely function, accompanied the vision.

His memory shot forward to that horrible night in St. Louis cemetery no. 1. The only time he remembered it was in his dreams—this dream. He could feel Lottie's neck in his hands, feel her terror, feel her flesh give as his knife slid across her throat, feel the pleasure as her blood trickled over his knuckles.

She got what she deserved. Just like her ancestor, that bitch that killed Laurent.

Julien's heart thundered in his chest when he woke, sweat coating his skin and saturating the linens.

"Jesus," he muttered, kicking off the sopping sheet strangling him. "Fuck me."

He sat on the edge of the bed for a moment hoping his heart would ease up. It was like a goddamn sauna in the room, a fucking inferno.

He needed a drink and a smoke and one of those little "chill the eff out" pills his doctor had prescribed.

Grabbing the goods, he headed to the porch. The night air was muggy but somehow cooler than the stagnant, air conditioned staleness he'd left behind in the cabin. Must be that whole, "fresh air" bullshit people raved about.

That fucking dream. It was the same over and over, and had been plaguing him since that fateful week so many months ago. And every time, he felt like he'd been rung out, hung out, and left to wither in the sun. The emotions of the dream were so real, it was hard to tell where they left off and he began.

He wasn't sure which medicine he needed most, so he lit a cigarette, and then downed the Valium with a shot of Beam, immediately followed by a drag on the cigarette that practically went to the butt.

His heart immediately slowed a good thirty beats per minutes. He let out a sigh. "That's the shit." The medicine might be all placebo but he didn't give a fuck. When he needed it, he needed it. And he was sure as hell never without it. All three. He wasn't even that much of a smoker, but something about the little cancer stick was calming in these situations.

Unfortunately the trifecta was needed a couple times a week. He'd always looked to alcohol to quiet that nagging voice in his head reminding him of what a dipshit he was, and letting him forget the ass load of failures. It'd been years since drugs were necessary. But after Lottie, he couldn't get to the doctor fast enough. He could have went the illegal route, but he was at least grown up enough to know that was a horrible idea.

He finished the cigarette and then worked on the Beam while the Valium throttled down his heartbeat to a more sensible pace.

The sound of a woman screaming sent it back into overdrive. It came from Nichole's cabin.

He practically dropped the Beam when he set it on the end table. Leaping off the porch in a single bound, he crossed the short distance between the cabins before launching his body onto her porch.

He rapped on the door with quick, sharp blows. A single candle burning inside was promptly blown out, but after that nothing moved. He knocked on the door again. "Nichole? You okay?"

He waited a few moments. When no one answered, he pressed his ear to the wood. He could hear the air conditioner working but nothing else. He knocked a final time, harder and with more force. Fuck if he was going to let her blow him off again.

"Nichole! Answer the damn door."

Why the hell did he care so much? She'd already made it clear she didn't give two shits about him. But his feet wouldn't let him off this porch until he knew she was at least breathing.

He was about to knock again, this time with enough force to break the thing down if need be, when the door finally creaked open.

Nichole peeked through the tiny slit. Even though he could only see a sliver of her face, what was visible looked frightened, wary, and he could clearly see the whites of her eyes.

"What?" she asked.

"I heard you scream. Just making sure everything is okay."

She glanced over her shoulder. "Yeah, it's fine. I'm fine. Thanks."

She started to close the door and he threw a hand out to stop her. "You don't look fine. Do you need any help?"

Her expression cycled between shock and bewilderment, before returning to wariness. "No, I'm fine. I just saw a...spider."

"Must have been some spider."

"Huge."

"I do have rather big feet. Need me to kill it?"

The bewilderment returned. "No. I, um, took care of it." She glanced over her shoulder again. "It's gone."

"Okay. Well if you need—"

"I'll be sure to fetch you," she interrupted. "Um, thanks, Julien."

"Anyti—" The door closed on his sentence.

"All righty then," he mumbled to the closed door. He really had no clue what to think about that girl. No. Clue.

But at least the Valium was kicking in and he would probably be able to sleep the night away in a calmed, Beam and downer coma.

And if he were completely honest, he was thankful for the distraction. Worrying about her problems let him forget about his.

Giving Voodoo tours in New Orleans late into the night meant bright and early for Julien was about ten a.m. By the time he rolled up to the main house at noon, it was bustling with activity. Not from guests, but staff hustled about, obviously prepping for *something*. Including Miss Puts.

He followed after her for a while as she waddled about barking orders. "What can I do for you, honey?" she finally asked when he fell in line beside her. "Leroy! Don't put that table there! It goes on the back veranda!"

"Do you have a wedding today or something?"

"No, darlin'. Alligator fry." She stopped short in the middle of a large room that had probably been a ballroom at one time. Now it was obviously event space. "Not the white tablecloths, you idiots! The black ones! This is s'posed to be a memorial!" She pushed through French doors and onto the veranda on the back of the house. A large tent and several smaller ones had been erected on the lawn.

Had he heard right? Surely not…

"Alligator fry…and memorial?" he asked as he followed her outside.

She turned to him as she made her way down the stairs. "Yessir. Seven this evenin'. Everybody's invited and everybody'll be here. It's just a little something we're puttin' together for Nichole's daddy." She wrinkled her nose in smug satisfaction. "A little revenge dinner."

What a horrible idea. Even Julien had enough social grace to realize what bad taste that was. Poor Nichole. Her father's body was barely cold. Well, assuming there was actually a body somewhere.

"Don't let the memorial fool ya. It's gonna be a good time. Band, food, drinks… The plantation spared no expense."

"I'll keep it in mind." To avoid, he added silently.

"What are you doing?" Miss Puts' shrill voice made him wince. She stormed over to a couple of young workers unfolding plastic tables under one of the smaller tents. There were dozens of them. This was an event meant for hundreds of people. He supposed it was a nice gesture to Nichole's father, even it was tacky.

"I told you, tables go this way!" She gestured wildly with her thick arms. "Not this way!" She gestured again, the hanging folds of skin flapping back and forth, making it look like she could take flight at any moment.

"Idiots," she muttered as she walked away. "It's so hard to find good help," she said to him. She was already hustling toward another group of workers, no doubt ready to bark out more orders.

"Miss Puts, I only really need about five minutes of your time and I'll be out of your hair."

"Sure, sugar. But only five minutes. I got lots to take care of." She stopped at looked at him expectantly, though her eyes continued to dart about.

"How much do you know about the history of this plantation?"

"All of it," she replied with confidence.

"Good." He attempted to make his smile sincere. He was actually glad to hear she was the resident expert. He simply couldn't seem to give the old bag a genuine smile. "Because I'm not actually here for vacation. I'm here for research." Pulling out the pictures of the Grisé sisters, he showed them to her. "Do you recognize these women?"

She barely glanced at them. "No."

"That's interesting because the surname is listed as Grisé. And in 1840, when the pictures were taken, this was the only Grisé household in Louisiana."

"Those women ain't no Grisés."

He purposefully flipped the pictures over. "No, it distinctly says Grisé. These were found in my deceased Grandmere's room. Don't know why she'd make up the name…?"

Puts laughed. "Well, honey, don't know what to tell you. Those mulatto girls can't be Grisés. This is my family home. I'm a Grisé by birth, and I know there aren't any mixed people in my family."

"Mulatto?" There was no hiding the shock in his voice. Outside of a textbook, he didn't think he'd ever heard that word spoken aloud. "You barely looked at the pictures. How the hell can you tell from a two second glance?" He held up one of the photos. "Especially since this woman is pretty damn white."

Once again, she barely glanced at it. "Oh no, honey, I can always tell." She winked.

Well, his mixed ancestry was obvious, so no big surprise there.

"Is that all you needed, sweetie?"

"Yeah," he said dryly.

"Well come back tonight and have a beer and some gator. Should be a damn fine time." She winked again before turning and puttering off back toward the house.

That conversation convinced him of absolutely nothing except Miss Puts was a racist kook. Of course, that wasn't a shocker or anything either.

Back to square one.

Since he was pretty sure the Grisé sisters were somehow tied to his family *and* this plantation, he decided to spend the rest of the afternoon photographing the place. He might need pictures for his book, and now was as good a time as any to collect them.

CHAPTER SEVEN

Edges of sunlight peeked through the curtains and flickered across her face, blinking in and out with regular frequency. Chirping faintly, the ceiling fan swirled above, making tiny gusts in her loose hair. The blanket had been tossed on the floor sometime in the early morning hours and now only a sheet covered her bare shoulders.

She'd abandoned the idea of sleep hours ago, but last night had taken a toll. Making contact and the mental assault that followed pushed her over the edge of exhaustion and at eleven a.m., she was still in bed.

The last failed attempts at more sleep crumbled when the obnoxiously loud ringer of the phone on the nightstand jolted her upright. Reaching and then fumbling for the receiver, she caught it just it before it crashed to the floor.

"H...hello?" she whispered with gargled words, wincing and grabbing at her head as tight pain squeezed her brain.

"Nichole? Honey? You awake, child?" Puts' shrill voice screamed in her ear, causing the pain in her head to spark.

She grimaced. "Yeah, I'm...I'm up."

"Honey, you still sleepin', ain't cha? It's shrimp boil day! We already on the bang-bang about settin' everything up. Wendell's loading up supplies. He's gonna make you keep your promise to help. We got somethin' special planned for you."

She nodded and let out a sigh. "Yeah, okay, give me thirty minutes." And a pot of coffee and a handful of ibuprofen. It felt like she'd drank a couple bottles of red wine last night. "Tell Wendell to keep his shirt on."

"Girl, you tell him. I ain't goin' near him. He's a crabby S.O.B. today. You just best hurry up, ya hear? Besides, you stayin' in bed milkin' your daddy's death ain't gonna do you no good."

Her heart clenched with sudden grief. She swallowed her indignation. "I'm not milking anything, Puts—"

"I seen the lights on after midnight at your daddy's place. I know it's hard to ease your mind, but you gotta move on, child. He's with Jesus now."

Blood flamed her cheeks as her jaw clenched tight. "I gotta go." She slammed the receiver into the cradle. Her hands flew to her face.

I will not cry, I will not cry...

Her head throbbed again, pain pushing the tears aside. God, what was it with this headache? It had to be from the failed contact. If being surrounded by dozens of corpses wasn't a big enough deterrent to opening herself up to the spirits constantly surrounding her, this sure was.

At least she'd been able to shut them out.

She knew she'd need to try again, but it was the last thing she wanted to think about, especially with this dagger in her brain.

So she wouldn't. Nor would she think about what happened in the swamp yesterday, or how she'd ditched Julien, or how her father's disappearance was still unsolved. She'd help with the boil like she'd promised (more like been roped into) when she first arrived and worry about the other things later.

After downing three full glasses of water and enough ibuprofen to make a horse forget its broken leg, she took nearly forty minutes making sure she didn't look like the wreck she was before joining Wendell in the old barn that served as a supply shed, home for the tractor and landscaping equipment, and the grounds keeper's office—Daddy's office.

"'Bout time you showed up," Wendell grumbled, wiping sweat from his brow. "Grab that table over there for the shrimp." He pointed inside the building.

Her eyes followed the gesture. "I see it."

"Then help me finish loadin' up these chairs."

Wendell was as crotchety as they came, and definitely too old to be doing this kind of work. Since he was Puts' brother and co-owner of the plantation, she'd known him since she was little. Even then he was old. And crotchety. But he was a good man. His only remaining job was working the riding mower and cutting the grass around the plantation, so she would suck it up for him. Especially since this would normally be Daddy's job.

It wasn't that hot out yet, but it had to be over one hundred degrees in the dimly lit shed. The intense heat took her breath away and brought out an instant sheen of sweat all over her body, making her grateful that she wore an old pair of shorts and white tank.

Halfway into the inferno, she paused and called out over her shoulder, "The table all you need, Wendell?"

"For the moment, there's some—" He was cut off by Miss Puts' loud command.

"Y'all be sure and grab those string lights, too. Better to light the way for the drunks then to let one of 'em fall right into Bubba's mouth."

She winced at the sound of the woman's voice as much as her words. With a shake of her head and a narrowing of her eyes, she gave Puts the middle finger.

Puts might not have a filter, but the insensitive remarks were starting to get to her. For all her claims of adoring Daddy and knowing him longer than anyone else, Puts sure didn't seem bothered by his *death*. In fact, she seemed to be reveling in the attention she, and the plantation, were getting.

Swallowing her spite like she always did, Nichole dragged the table to the grassy area next to the tractor, leaning it against the barn beside the stacks of chairs. Surprisingly, Puts had already wandered off. Which was good. She really didn't want to deal with any more of the woman's *concerned* comments.

Panting, his face bright red, Wendell leaned heavily against the chairs already stacked on the trailer hitched behind the tractor.

"Wendell? I got that table. Want me to grab the lights?"

"Yeah... They're back..." he panted, "....on...the shelves..."

"Wendell, you okay? Why don't I go grab Shay?"

"He's buyin' a...all the shrimps down at Landaiche's. H...he not be back for another hour or so." His breathing so labored, he puffed loudly between words.

Her mouth turned down a little. "Maybe you should take a load off, Wendell, before heat stroke do you in." Her frown deepened. The Louisiana accent was getting thicker by the second. It was something she'd worked hard to eliminate, careful to always enunciate and never skip words. But being back at the plantation was making that difficult.

"Nonsense."

"C'mon," she said, taking his sweaty hand. "Humor me."

"Oh, I'm all right," Wendell insisted, waving his free hand as though shooing away a swarm of gnats.

She reluctantly let go of him. "At least let me grab you some water."

"Sure, girl. Grab them lights while you're in there."

There was a refrigerator in the office, which thankfully was air conditioned. Any relief from the heat she enjoyed while retrieving the water was instantly reversed as she rummaged through the shelves looking for packed away Christmas lights. If she'd been thinking, she would have done the tasks in reverse, getting the lights first before water.

Wendell was sitting on one of the plastic chairs, still mopping sweat from his body when she returned to the somewhat cooler outdoors. Unfolding one from the stack against the shed, she sat beside him, handing him the water.

"Ruby is right, you know," Wendell said out of the blue. "Your daddy ain't comin' back and there ain't no reason for you to be hidin' in that cottage, sleeping for days."

At first she was annoyed by the uninvited and intrusive comment, but the expression on his weathered face and the genuine tone in his voice said he was truly worried for her.

"I miss him," she admitted softly. "How can you not miss him too?"

His eyes narrowed. "You listen to me, missy. I taught your daddy everything he know 'bout this plantation. Spent months showing him the lay of the land and more months landscapin' it. And then all them cottages..." He nodded in their direction. "Took years to get 'em restored." His face scrunched up and he looked away. "You think it easy for me to lose him? That I don't grieve?"

She was pretty sure his voice broke, but since it was normally filled with so much gravel it was hard to be sure. Elbows resting on his thighs, he continued to stare out into the distance. Finally, he gave his knees a slap. "Whelp, I got a job to do. People dependin' on me. Ain't nothing gonna make this old man look weak."

He went to rise and then struggled to get all the way to his feet. Popping up out of the chair, she applied enough gentle pressure to help him all the way up.

"Guess I might just be a weak old man after all. I might be too old to work, but I'm gonna keep pushing myself 'til the good Lord want me back."

"Nonsense." She squeezed his hand and felt a slight tightening in return. "All right," she said with a faint tremor in her voice, "time to get back to it."

Tying to remain inconspicuous, she made a conscious effort to do most of the work herself from that point on. Wendell seemed content to sit back and bark out orders, which was pretty much perfect.

A dilapidated 1970s truck with a windshield full of spider cracks and fenders with more rust than metal was waiting for them at the shed as they pulled up the tractor after delivering the chairs to the manor. Two men stood beside the truck, a tarp strung between them. Judging from the way it bowed in the middle, something heavy was wrapped inside. Like a body.

"Well, I'll be," Wendell murmured. "Looks like the Villeres came through after all."

She stared at the two men. Of course! That's where she'd heard the name Villere. They were a backwoods family living deep in the bayou. She immediately wondered if they were any relation to Julien and then quickly dismissed it. No way. These people were as inbred as they came.

The family kept to themselves, so she didn't really know the older man, but she definitely recognized the younger one, Eugene, a.k.a. Two-Tooth. They were about the same age, and even though he'd never attended a day of public school—he was supposedly home schooled—she'd seen him around from time to time during her youth.

Two-Tooth was a nickname he received due to the minimal amount of remaining teeth in his mouth. Of those, the front were as buck as two could get. He also had a reputation for being unbelievably stupid. Rumor had it the Villeres rarely married outside their family, which would explain Two-Tooth's unfortunate genetics.

He must have recognized her too, because he aimed a snaggletooth yet dubious smile directly at her—revealing a mash-up of puke-yellow grime and gritty, black chewing tobacco. Equally disgusting were his overalls, which he wore without a shirt, highlighting a pair of man-boobs rivaling her own. Blood and dirt splatters were streaked across his flesh, like he'd just returned from a murderous rampage.

He not only creeped her out, he downright revolted her.

Wendell killed the tractor motor, his joints creaking loudly as he climbed to the ground.

"Put m over there, Norbert," he said.

The older man looked sheepishly in Wendell's direction and then over at her, leering a little longer than was comfortable. She felt the hairs on her forearm rising and glanced over at Wendell, wondering if he noticed, but his facial expression never changed.

Norbert and Two-Tooth walked toward the grassy spot Wendell had indicated. Whatever was causing the bulging bow in the tarp swayed with a heft that indicated it easily weighed couple hundred pounds. She hoped the "'em" wasn't actually a "him."

"You got a big 'un didn't you?"

"Mmm," Norbert grumbled, his head tilted down.

The truck door opened and a woman stepped out. She might have been all of one hundred pounds, with scraggly gray hair and a faded floral print dress clearly overstating her unfortunate decision not to wear a bra. "Where's Robert?" she asked.

"Ain't here right now, Brigitte. I'll take it." Wendell limped toward her, wiping his sweaty face with a bandana.

"Here ya go," she said with a smile, handing Wendell what looked like a receipt. She had considerably more teeth than Two-Tooth, though they were gray with age. "We can cut 'em up or you can take 'em to Gator Getters," she said. "Yer choice, but it'll be an extra fifty and we keepin' the skins."

"Best if y'all do it. We're short on time as it is."

Brigitte nodded. "Lay 'em open, boys," she said to the men beside her.

The tarp flopped onto the ground, plastic falling open to reveal a large, limp alligator.

"Best get a couple coolers and some ice," she said.

"Nichole," Wendell called, "mind runnin' into the shed and grabbin' a couple coolers and some ice?"

"Sure," Nichole answered meekly. She climbed down from the tractor, her gaze glued on Norbert as he handed a knife to Two-Tooth.

They weren't planning on butchering that animal right there, were they? Not only was the idea revolting, but both those knives seemed relatively small for the job; one was about ten inches long with a skinny blade, the other shorter and more compact.

As she walked past the makeshift butcher station, Two-Tooth flipped the beast onto its back and Norbert shoved his knife into its belly. It made the most God awful crunching sound. Closing her eyes she turned her head, holding her lips tightly shut.

"Don't trouble over it, girl," Wendell said. "They too many in the swamps already."

"Oh, I'm not troubling over it. I'm trying to keep from hurling." It wasn't like she'd never seen an animal butchered. Daddy often cleaned his own kills. But there was something about *this* animal being butchered by *these* people.

The oppressive heat inside the shed was a welcome escape from the scene outside. She didn't even mind the sweat beading up on her forehead and dripping into her eyes as she picked through storage totes to gather a couple coolers. Anything to distract her from the sound of ripping flesh drifting through the open doors. She dragged the coolers into the office, carefully closing the door behind her.

Happy to be in air conditioning and with a wall separating her from the revulsion outside, she took her time emptying every single ice tray in the office fridge into the coolers. It wasn't until the last piece of ice broke free from its plastic prison that the realization of what was happening hit her like a brick wall.

Every drop of moisture was sucked from her mouth, and she had to grab the freezer edge to steady her feet.

Oh, God! This wasn't just some random delivery for the restaurant. This was for the shrimp boil! The one to honor her supposed deceased father—a man everyone thought had been eaten by an effing alligator. They were actually going to *serve* alligator.

Holy hell. Of all the tactless things...

Boiling blood burned her ears. Slamming the freezer door shut, she scooped up the coolers, anger making the weight and awkwardness of carrying two coolers layered with rattling ice irrelevant.

Marching out of the office and then out of the shed, she dropped the coolers on the ground next to Wendell.

"You could have told me," she whispered harshly to him.

His eyes flicked to her. "Told you what?"

"You didn't think it would bother me if a few pounds of alligator were fried up for Daddy's memorial?" She was having a hard time keeping her voice low. "Like some sort of revenge feast? His body wouldn't even be digested yet."

"I thought you knew." Wendell's look of confusion calmed her down a bit. And it also confirmed that it was Miss Puts' insensitive, ridiculous idea. Sometimes that woman was unbelievable.

"No! But I guess I should have," she muttered bitterly. "Only Puts..." Would be this inappropriate, she finished silently. It would be bad manners to curse the woman aloud, especially to her own brother, so Nichole bit her tongue.

"Ruby means well," Wendell said.

She forced a smile to her face. "Of course."

The idea of marching up to the plantation manor and telling Ruby "Puts" Grisé off crossed her mind more than once in the four seconds of silence that followed. It would serve the woman right, but Nichole knew it wouldn't do any good. Logic would never get through the hair spray helmet. But, still...this?

Her headache came back with a pounding vengeance.

A noise that sounded like boots being sucked off by mud came from behind her and, like an idiot, she turned around. The scene was straight out of a horror movie. There was blood everywhere, and entrails, and...blood. Two-Tooth was busily—and skillfully—filleting pieces of white flesh while Norbert peeled off the alligator's skin in one smooth piece. Brigitte leaned against the truck and watched the macabre activities wearing a peculiar smile that almost looked like an expression of delight.

Jesus, who actually enjoyed watching this?

Tasting bile, Nichole clutched her stomach and turned away. She couldn't be here anymore. Between the slaughterhouse behind her, the sickness of the situation, the heat, and the ramifications of her failed attempts to find out information about Daddy from the ghost world, she couldn't take any more. Promise or not, she was done.

"I, uh...I gotta go," she managed.

"Of course, Nikki," Wendell said, his tone surprisingly soft. "Rest up. You got a long night ahead."

She tried to keep her gaze directed at the path before her feet, but her stupid peripheral vision took in the scene without her permission. She couldn't tell her brain to stop fast enough.

Bayou Grisé: Sins of Sanite

The leftover carcass and entrails were a red, goopy mess. Brigitte stood at the edge of the tarp, spraying water over the blue plastic with the hose, making the blood run off in vigorous red rivers. She didn't even want to know what Norbert and Two-Tooth were doing. Still clutching her stomach, she pushed her stride out as far as it would go. She couldn't get back to the cabin fast enough.

The cool, familiar darkness of her cabin combined with a nice, cold shower helped soothe her anger and calm her mind, allowing her to consider everything with a clearer head.

Yes, serving alligator at a memorial for her father was in bad taste, but Puts *was* putting up quite an effort, not to mention expense, to host it. Maybe it was because she simply liked the attention, or because she liked being recognized for being gracious, but no matter the motive, it was still a thoughtful gesture, like Wendell said.

Still wet, dripping water, and wrapped in a towel, she stood at her closet door, staring at the measly contents. The sudden news of Daddy's death resulted in minimal preparation in the apparel department. Luckily she'd left several items behind during her last visit. Flipping through the few neatly hung items, she chose a loose sleeveless blouse, the cream fabric thin and perfect for an oppressively humid Louisiana night. Blue jean shorts and simple brown sandals kept the outfit casual.

If anything, Puts' insensitive actions made Nichole think about her own selfishness. After all, only twenty-four hours earlier she'd completely abandoned a guest of the plantation in a potentially dangerous situation. A man who, no matter how annoying, appeared to be concerned for her welfare. Not only had she abandoned him, she'd hid from him like an insensitive child when his concern led him to her door. And later, he'd still checked up on her--In the middle of the night even.

She owed him an apology. Walking over to the bed, she stared at the phone. Should she…call him?

She picked up receiver and pushed the number eight before she could change her mind. It connected right away and started to ring. Her hands were already getting clammy waiting for Julien to answer. She hoped it would keep ringing and give her enough time to figure out what to say to him.

A woman's recorded voice promptly picked up. Four rings? That was all she got?

"Cottage eight guests are unavailable," the voice cooed. "Please leave a message at the beep."

She almost hung up, but decided to get it over with. Now was as good a time as any.

"Hey Julien, it's me, Nichole." She hesitated for a moment, mentally trying to prep the right words. "Listen, I know this is short notice, but the plantation is having a shrimp boil tonight and I'd…um…" She paused, the apology stuck at the back of her throat. "I thought you might like to go. Free drinks and food seem like something you'd be into." With a grimace, she rolled her eyes. Some apology. "Anyway, I wasn't sure if anyone had let you know. I'll be there and—"

A loud beep interrupted, causing her to wince.

Shit. Should she call him back?

She stared at the receiver before carefully hanging up. Screw it. He'd either show up or not, and it was already six and her hair was a wet, stringy mess that needed taming if she was going to feel remotely in control. She'd deal with Julien later.

CHAPTER EIGHT

The shrimp boil was going strong by eight-thirty. As soon as the sun started going down and the air cooled, even if the difference happened to be minuscule, people came out in droves, converging on the plantation like a swarm of grasshoppers. Every neighbor within a thirty mile radius, as well as plantation guests, settled around the tables of free food and drink like hogs at a trough.

Set a ways back from the partygoers, the boilers and outdoor fryers were in full force, kicking up extra heat and steam as batch after batch of shrimp hit the boiling water and battered alligator was dipped into hot grease.

The mere thought of the latter was nauseating.

Just like at the wake, Nichole put on her best smile and made her rounds as was expected, choking back her disgust over the situation. Even though they happily stuffed their faces and filled their bellies with free food and alcohol, the local guests seemed to realize how inappropriate the festivities were. They avoided her like she was a leper, even going so far as turning away if she walked by.

That was fine with her. She didn't really want to talk to anyone anyway. She hadn't seen a hint of Julien Villere, and she hated to admit, she was somewhat relieved. No matter how much he might deserve her apology, it was something she was dreading.

So to keep isolated while still maintaining the necessary party presence, she made herself busy by cleaning up empty beer bottles and making sure trash was properly disposed of. It was a thankless task, but at least it kept her occupied.

By ten o'clock, the band belted out amped up tunes and everything and everyone got a little louder and a little rowdier. Cajuns definitely liked to party. She, however, was ready to sneak away. If nothing else for the fewer decibels she'd be relishing in her own bed. Beat didn't begin to describe her. More like run over by a Mack truck.

When she finally did commit to leaving, she turned and saw Julien Villere approaching—making a beeline straight toward her. And judging by the determined way he walked, he wanted answers.

"Shit," she whispered under her breath, cringing both outwardly and inwardly. Time to face the music…

Even though she'd been mentally prepping her apology all night in case she did see him, now that the moment of reckoning was upon her, she froze. What *was* she supposed to say to him again? Sorry I ditched you and then hid in my house when you knocked...

"Well, if it isn't the disappearing track star," he said when he reached her.

She couldn't quite tell by his tone whether he was joking or angry. He might even be both.

"Hey," she managed, guilt warming her cheeks. "You made it."

"With such a stellar invitation via garbled voicemail, how could I not show?" Grinning, the low light barely showed the gleam in his eyes. It was definitely there though.

He *was* teasing. For some reason, knowing he wasn't angry made her relax. Though she still needed to choke out that apology.

"Listen, about last night, I'm so—"

"Hold that thought," he interrupted, lifting a hand. "Let's have a drink first."

"Wine and beer are over there." She gestured toward the troughs filled with ice, beer, and soda. Boxes of wine sat next to pitchers of sweet tea on adjacent tables.

"Lead the way."

She did and he followed, staying a few steps behind her. When she turned to see what was making him hesitate, she caught him checking out her ass.

Stopping to cross her arms tightly against her chest, she tilted her head in question. The cocky bastard just winked.

"There are some things a man just can't help," he told her as he passed.

"I think you can."

Still striding toward the beer tent, he tossed over his shoulder, "No, I can't."

Her arms fell away as she shook her head. What an arrogant—

Oh, um...yeah. He had a pretty nice ass too.

Rolling her eyes at herself, she jogged to catch up.

It was quieter over by the refreshments. Miss Puts intentionally kept the alcohol some distance away from everyone and everything. She seemed to like making guests work a little harder for their buzz. Though it was probably best. If the liquor were anywhere near the band, most of the partygoers would probably already be passed out drunk—the locals anyway.

Shockingly, they were the only ones in the tent. Even though Nichole had spent the entire evening keeping things tidied up, the table was in shambles. Wine had been spilled all over the black linen and beer bottles haphazardly tossed about.

They reached into the trough at the same time and their hands touched. She met his gaze as they both slowly pulled back. His eyes said it all. He liked touching her.

She cleared her throat.

"I pegged you for a wine girl," he said, twisting off his beer cap.

She did the same. "Please." She took a long drink. "I grew up in a damn swamp. Of course I like beer. Especially when it's ice cold and hot as sin outside."

His lips curled up into a grin. Holding out his bottle, he said, "Cheers."

She met the glass with her own. "Cheers." They both took drinks.

"Want to sit somewhere?" he asked.

Actually, she did. "Yeah. There's some seating in the food tent."

"I can always eat."

As tall, broad shouldered, and muscular as he was, she didn't doubt that for a second.

The drink tent might have been empty, but the food tent was definitely not. The entire party seemed to be crowded around the numerous tables, surrounded by food and more food. Plates were piled high with gator, shrimp, potatoes, and corn.

They managed to score a couple chairs tucked away in the corner.

"I feel like we got off on the wrong foot," Julien said as they sat.

He definitely wasn't a man who was light with his words. His bluntness was actually refreshing. The plantation was sometimes a culture of pleasantries on the surface and backstabbing snarkiness in the background.

"You could say that."

"Well, now that we're even, we can start off fresh."

"Even?"

"Yeah. I say something totally inappropriate about your father's wake, you ditch me in the swamp. Seems like an even trade to me. I mean, there was the risk of death for me, but," he shrugged, "still seems pretty even to me."

She rolled her eyes again. "There wasn't a risk of death…" Much of a risk, anyway.

"Okay, maybe just the risk of screaming like a little girl out of pure fright. Close enough." He held out his hand. "So, fresh start?"

Lips pursed together to keep from laughing out loud, she took his hand. A big, solid hand. It lacked the calluses of a man that worked with them, but was no less strong.

"Julien Villere."

"Nichole Montoya."

"Ah, Montoya… Any relation to Inigo? Ever find that six-fingered man?"

"Ha, ha. Ha. Ha... Ha."

He grinned. "So you've never heard that one?"

"No. Never."

"Of course not," he said with a wink. "I'm an original. Julien the Witty Villere is my nickname back home."

"You mean Julien the Dim-Witty Villere."

He winked again. "You got it."

She took a drink just to avoid laughing. For some reason, he didn't press on anything. He didn't seem to want an actual apology, or need an explanation. He appeared to be happy just to sit and have a beer with her. No anger, no questions. How was it possible for him to just...accept?

Partygoers filtered in and out of the tent. The band was set up far enough away that the twang of the fiddle was softened. They enjoyed a few more beers and light conversation focused mainly around Nichole and what she did in Baton Rouge—a buyer for a high-end department store. Totally boring, but a nice break from the chaos of the last few days.

She felt considerably more relaxed than she had all evening, maybe even since she arrived. Julien had an easy charm about him. Conversation seemed to be one of his strengths. He knew all the right questions to ask to keep the words flowing, even with the din of dozens of voices surrounding them.

Beer number three was keeping her hands cold when one of the many locals she'd rather not be around lumbered into the tent with his brother in tow and a sloshing beer in hand. He went to the food table and filled a paper plate with alligator before his half-lidded, three-sheets-to-the-wind gaze fell on her. He thoroughly took her in from head to toe, lingering a tad too long for comfort. He then caught sight of Julien, sized him up, snarled a little, and set his food and beer on the nearest table with a thud.

In the stupidity of her youth, they'd actually dated one summer. Back then, he'd been able to charm her with his muscles and thick-headed simplicity. And she was a vapid teenager trying to escape her own problems. Hormones and a lack of experience outside of rural Louisiana were a poor combination for good decision making.

Very purposefully looking their direction, the tank-top-clad behemoth picked up a large piece of fried alligator, looked at it, and said rather dramatically, "Hello, my name is Nichole Montoya. You killed my father. Prepare to die." He then finished the entire strip of fried meat in one disgusting swallow.

Julien turned to her, his face filled with disbelief and shock. "Do you know that idiot?"

She nodded reluctantly. "Yeah, that's Jean Thibodeaux. The other idiot with him is his brother, Dean."

"Jean and Dean. Nice." His expression softened. "I'm so sorry for my joke earlier," he said sincerely.

"It's fine. You didn't mean it the same way."

"It is not fine. And neither is this." He turned back to the brothers. "Hey, Jethro. Is something fucking wrong with you?"

Jean slowly lowered the piece of fish he was about to stuff into his face. "You talkin' to me?"

"Yeah, I'm talking to you," Julien said, rising from the chair. "Are you mentally slow or something?"

"No…"

"Well, you aren't fucking twelve. That was wholly inappropriate. You need to apologize to the lady."

"Who the fuck are you?"

Julien closed the distance between them, his posture erect, his broad chest lifted. There was no questioning his intent. He was ready to throw down.

"Julien Villere," he said slowly, his New Orleans accent thick and so different than the bayou drawl. "But right now, you can think of me as your daddy, because you're about to get your ass whooped if you don't apologize."

"What, you think you can make me?"

Dean puffed up behind Jean, clearly ready to have his brother's back.

Julien stepped even closer until the distance between him and Jean were mere inches. The top of Jean's head only came to Julien's collarbone. The closeness made the height difference glaringly obvious as Julien bent his head to look down and Jean had to crane his to look up.

"I'm pretty sure that won't be a problem. Now, grow some pipsqueak balls and apologize before I knock your little pea head off."

Jean paused and Julien cocked his head. He puffed his chest out further, nearly bumping Jean's nose with his pecs.

Finally, Jean stepped back. "Sorry, Nichole. Just a little harmless joke."

"Sure, Jean. No problem."

The brothers glared at Julien a final time before skulking away.

"Thanks for defending my honor," she said when Julien rejoined her.

"Any time. Hey, you want to get out of here?"

She gave him a once over, seeing him in a new light. Cocky? Yes. Arrogant? Obviously. But maybe his declarations of chivalry weren't just smoke signals after all.

Yeah, she did want to get out of there. She definitely did.

"There's a gazebo over by the pond." She started to gesture, when out of the blue he took her hand and brought it to his lips.

"Perfect. I'll grab a few more beers and meet you back here." Bobbing his eyebrows at her, he released her hand and disappeared from the tent.

She could only stare in the direction he disappeared to. Did he just kiss her hand? Like it was the most natural act in the world? And did she like it?

The excitement swarming in her belly at the prospect of being alone with him confirmed that she did.

Holy hell. What was she doing?

Having a good time. Taking a mental break.

Chill out, she told herself. Even with everything going on, she deserved a little distraction. In fact, if she didn't divert her attention, she'd probably lose her mind.

Julien's large frame appeared at the edge of the tent. He held up the beers as invitation. That was all she needed, and the swarming excitement pushed her steps quickly toward him.

There wasn't a soul by the gazebo or pond. Located on the opposite end of the manicured plantation grounds, it was far enough away that the band and raucous party noise were faint distractions. Instead, insects buzzed around like happy music makers; lightning bugs flickering in and out provided extra mood lighting.

Sitting on the edge of the gazebo wooden railing, she invited Julien to do the same.

"Thanks again for standing up to Jean on my behalf."

"Of course. I wouldn't mind smacking that Miss Puts down a peg or two. I'm sorry, Nichole, but this whole 'alligator fry' must be awful for you."

She wrinkled her nose. "It's a little…off-putting, but I know Puts means well. For the most part."

He started to reply and then pushed his lips together and paused. Holding up the beers, he asked, "Ready for another?"

That wasn't what he planned to say, she was sure of it. Holding her bottle up to the dim light, she squinted. Less than an inch of liquid sloshed in the bottom. Tipping her head back, she open-mouthed the remainder and then set the empty down on the railing with a thud. "Sure."

He laughed, deep and from the belly, and passed over a beer. "Damn, girl. I sure had you pegged all wrong."

With a grin, she took the full beer and a fresh, healthy drink. "You know, I think I had you pegged wrong too. You just rubbed me a little…wrong, at first."

"No surprise. My mouth often runs ahead of my brain, especially when I'm trying to be clever or funny. Job hazard I suppose."

"Oh yeah, what do you do?"

"My family owns a Voodoo store. Besides occasionally fucking up the books by running it when my brother can't, I give Voodoo tours."

"That explains it."

"The amazing wit and easy charm?"

She bit her lip. "Actually, yeah."

A breeze gusted in off the water, ruffling the hair on her shoulders and filling the fabric of her blouse so it billowed, floating up and exposing her entire abdomen and probably the bottom of her bra. Full beer in hand, she fumbled to pull it down with an unreasonable amount of embarrassment. Julien quickly reached over and took her beer, allowing her to make herself decent.

"Thanks," she muttered, making sure all the right parts were covered before lifting her gaze.

His actions might have been polite and gentlemanly, his expression wasn't. Desire stirred in green eyes, set off by his thick lashes. Lashes that might have been light in pigment, but had so many strands they stood out as much darker.

God, that look. Those eyes. That amazing jaw. Those lips...

She wet hers with her tongue. His eyebrows briefly pushed together and she was pretty sure she heard him moan a little.

The muscles in her core tightened and she pushed her knees together.

Oh, hell.

Her lip pinched between her teeth again. Was she really thinking about going down this route? Now, of all times?

What the hell. Why not?

Leaning over, she captured his lips with hers, pressing their flesh together delicately. So warm, so soft... She extended the tip of her tongue to taste him, just a little.

The sound of glass hitting wood piggybacked on what was definitely a moan. His hand reached around her neck, pulling her in and deepening the kiss, using his tongue to gently but firmly gain entrance to her mouth.

All tension in her body simply melted away.

His lips expertly caressed hers, his tongue slowly and definitely sexually probing her mouth. She felt the heat build between her legs and quickly spread until she was pretty sure she was twice as hot and definitely as damp as the air around them.

Never had a kiss, especially not a first kiss, felt so dirty. So hot. Nor had it held so many promises of pleasures to come.

A crack of thunder shook the gazebo, rattling the old wood and jostling her entire body. It was so loud, she was pretty sure the lightening must have struck nearby. Julien jerked back as well, knocking one of the beers off the railing. It landed with a definite slosh.

Lightening brightened the sky, a splintering bolt of white light cutting through the black moisture like a razor blade. Thunder immediately followed, so deafeningly loud she had to cover her ears.

She glanced at Julien.

"Think we should get out of this lightening rod?" he asked.

"Oh yeah. But as fast as this storm rolled in, I don't think we're going to make it without getting wet." She hadn't even seen storm clouds move in. Granted, the night was so dark, seeing anything but inky blackness would have been impossible.

"It'll be a wild ride. Ready?" Julien asked, holding out his hand. She took it with a nod and they bolted. They hadn't made it ten feet when the skies opened up, sending fat, drenching droplets of water careening to the ground.

By the time they reached the back porch of the main house, she was soaked and covered in splattered mud. She didn't even want to think about what her hair and makeup were doing.

Julien, however, looked pleasantly dewy. Raindrop rivulets did slide down his latte colored skin, but his short hair still looked perfectly groomed. And the waterlogged T-shirt clinging to every muscle on his chest, arms, and abs looked positively fine.

He grinned at her, breathing heavily from their sprint to the back veranda. "That was intense," he said.

She did her best to try and discretely wipe the mascara surely running down her cheeks. "Definitely." A swipe over her hair probably did nothing but ruffle any escaping curls.

"Relax, Nichole. You look great." He glanced around. Several dozen of the partygoers huddled under the shelter of the porch roof as the rain continued to pound the earth. He turned back to her. "I think we're stuck here for a while. And unfortunately, I'm pretty sure we lost any hope of privacy."

"Yeah..." A little heat rushed to her face. Considering the temperature had dropped a good twenty degrees and her wet skin actually felt a bit chilled, the flush felt intense.

Taking her hand, Julien led her toward an empty table, grabbing a couple glasses of wine set out on the portable bar.

Gusts of wind blew rain onto the porch in sporadic bursts so even the chairs were wet. It didn't matter at this point, since there wasn't a dry part on her body. And after that kiss, the statement was quite literal.

Julien handed her the wine. "Here's to good old fashioned, rain soaked, inappropriately themed parties in the bayou."

"And letting go of initial prejudices."

Their glasses clinked. "I can definitely drink to that."

She watched his eyes linger on her mouth as she took a sip. How wonderful would it be to forget everything and pick up where they left off in the gazebo, shoving the wine and centerpiece to the floor, reaching across the table, and just disappearing once again into that passionate kiss?

How wonderful indeed.

Her body language must have given away her desires, because the lust was back in his eyes. He shifted uncomfortably.

Oh God, did that mean—

She cleared her throat. "You know, I never asked," she started, keeping her focus on the swirling wine in her glass, "what brought you here?"

"Would you believe I'm writing a book?"

She began to laugh but stopped herself when his face dropped. "Oh... You're serious. I'm sorr—"

He shrugged it off, leaning back in his chair, one arm draped like wilted spinach over the back while the other held the wine loosely in his hand. "No worries," he said, amusement drenching his features. "No way you could have known. Besides, I enjoy shocking pretty girls."

Where she'd once found his cockiness irritating, now she found it completely sexy. She'd probably always found it sexy, hence why she'd found it irritating.

"Tell me about it. The book, I mean."

Taking a deep breath, he leaned closer as if it were a secret. "It's a book about Voodoo."

"Well, that makes sense considering your store. But it still doesn't answer my question. Why Plantation Grisé?"

"I found these pictures in my late Grandmere's room with the name Grisé on the back. She'd built shrines to them, Voodoo shrines, which makes no sense. I came here to figure out the connection."

"That's simple."

His brows pushed together. "How so?"

"You do know about the Villeres who live out in the swamp, don't you?"

"No." The crease between his brows deepened. "I don't."

"Norbert, Brigitte, and their son, Eugene. I wouldn't have dreamt you were related, but maybe you are. I can take you there tomorrow if you like."

"I thought I already knew every Villere in the state of Louisiana." He shook his head in bewilderment. "But sure," he winked, "take me to my people."

"God, the Swamp Villeres..." She cleared her throat. "Sorry, that's just what we've always called them—anyway, they look nothing like you. I'm pretty sure the combined number of teeth in the family is less than half of what you have."

His face was a mix of puzzlement and curiosity. "They sound positively charming. Now I *have* to meet them." He took a drink. "Wait, this doesn't have anything to do that crazy old man we saw out there yesterday, does it?"

She'd been so wrapped up in the idea of helping him out while being able to spend more time with him that she overlooked the *going into the swamp* part.

The White Eyes.

She shuddered.

Besides that the ghosts seems to be stronger in the bayou, *they* were there. The White Eyes. The ones she couldn't explain.

With that, everything rushed back and any semblance of peace and relaxation disappeared.

She shouldn't be here. She should be trying to figure out what happened to Daddy. She should be trying to gain enough strength to contact the dead again. She shouldn't be drinking the night away—no matter how much her frazzled nerves might need it.

"Is everything okay?"

Glancing up, she realized not only was she shivering, but she'd been staring blankly into the distance, toward the swamp and the ones that scared her the most. Concern was all over Julien's face.

Where at first she'd been annoyed that he seemed to know too much, now she didn't want him to know what she could do, what a freak of nature she was. She'd told people in the past. It hadn't ended well. Ghost Girl was the tamest nickname by far.

"I'm just cold, wet, and tired." All three were true, but it didn't explain the shivering.

"Well, it looks like the rain is starting to taper. Want me to escort you back to your cabin?"

She hesitated. Yes, she wanted him to walk her back. Actually, she'd like to return to the gazebo, return to the time and place where all she could think about was his flesh pressed against hers.

"Don't worry," he said, holding up his hands. "No funny business. In fact, I'll keep my hands in my pockets the entire time." He did so.

"Oh! No, um, no, it isn't...that. I just..." What the hell should she say? *I can see ghosts if I want to and need to contact them because they should know where my father is. I don't want to tell you though because I'm afraid you'll think I'm crazy, a freak, or both. And I sure as hell don't want to tell you what's really in that swamp...*

"I'll even keep my mouth shut," he went on. "No questions, no talking. Just let me walk you back."

How was he able to read her so well?

"Talking is fine," she said with a meek smile. Truly, she was a wreck and needed to end this night.

The rain had reduced to a drizzle. Storms rolled out just as fast as they rolled in—nobody knew when the next one would pop up. If she wanted to get back, she needed to go now.

Rising from the chair, she suddenly realized how revealing her wet blouse must be. It was Julien's expression that gave it away. Shit, it was probably completely see-through.

Sure enough, the saturated fabric clung to her flesh like a second skin, leaving nothing to the imagination. Luckily, she'd chosen a neutral bra in the same color as the blouse, so while it might be clearly visible, at least it wasn't leopard print.

Carefully, she pulled the fabric away from her skin. Of course the minute she released it, it just snapped right back into place.

"Girl, let's get out of here before you give every man in this place a heart attack."

He kept his word on the way back to the cabins, keeping the conversation light and simple. He told her a little more about his family's Voodoo shop and the guest house they ran. It was nice because it allowed her mind to focus on something other than, well, everything else.

He also kept his hands deep in his pockets. The gesture was sweet but unnecessary. She wouldn't mind having them on her again.

How could she think about that right now? She needed to focus on finding Daddy. And to do that, she needed to talk to the dead. And she sure as hell couldn't be distracted if she was going to contact them again. They'd get inside her head and never leave.

She reached the front door of her cabin before she realized Julien had stopped at the edge of the bottom step. Hands still in his pockets, he offered her a crooked smile.

"Goodnight, Nichole. Thanks for the invite," he said. "I had a great time."

She swallowed. He looked fabulous bathed in the pale porch light, with his see-through shirt and bedroom grin.

"Me too," she squeaked out.

Doorknob in her grasp, turned and ready to open, she paused. Could she tell him? Should she? Would it be like every other time?

Because of her abilities, Nichole had actually had very few relationships in her life. It was hard to know who to trust, who would take the news well, and who wouldn't run away scared.

In a split-second decision she released the door and bounded down to the bottom step, took his face in her hands, and kissed him quickly. One hand had just lifted from his pocket when she bounded back to the door.

"Goodnight," she said, this time pushing open the door. If she didn't go in, the night was going to go in a much different direction than it should. She needed to be inside. Daddy needed her inside.

"I'll see you tomorrow?" he wondered.

Yes. She could at least give him that. She might not be able to tell him the truth, or take him inside like she so desperately wanted, but she could give him a swamp tour and help him with his research. "Three o'clock. Meet me here."

"Looking forward to it."

She closed the door before she could change her mind.

CHAPTER NINE

Julien stood frozen in place for a good three minutes before he realized how stalkerish he must look standing at her stoop. Making a quick retreat to his own porch, he set up camp on one of the wicker chairs and tried not to look the direction of her cabin. Knowing the blinds were open made it far too tempting, and he busied his gaze with the swamp in the distance.

The night definitely hadn't gone the way he expected. Not in the least. Once he heard Nichole's voice message, he realized she might not despise him as much as she let on. But he never would have imagined the way things had gone, especially considering how poorly every other encounter went.

She'd kissed him. She'd actually fucking kissed him. Unbelievable.

Not that he was complaining, not even remotely. He might have picked up on some of her body language hints throughout the evening, but it had still surprised him. He never would have imagined she would be so forward. She seemed so…reserved.

Talk about a hot ass kiss. Like, instant erection, holy shit hot. Julien had plenty of access to girls. Being a tour guide in a city where everyone came to party and let loose made it easy to hook up with, well, loose women. So much so that it was possible being a tour guide in New Orleans was second only to being the lead singer in a band. It also helped that his tour hit multiple bars along the route.

He'd never denied he didn't take advantage of it. He was a dog, after all, and had been his entire life. There was no reason *not* to take advantage of it.

This was different. Way different. And better. However the fuck it happened.

Nichole was pent up passion. He could taste it on her tongue. It was like she was so used to holding back and keeping herself constantly restrained that she was dying to burst free. He'd give just about anything to be there when she did.

From the corner of his eye, he could tell she was rapidly moving about the house. Like the other day, she seemed to be searching for something. It was difficult to tell for sure from his limited perspective, and as tempting as it was to spy, he forced his gaze elsewhere. She deserved a little respect for her privacy. Hopefully tomorrow he could ask a few questions and actually get answers.

It was obvious she was hiding something. What, he wasn't sure, but he'd spent enough of his life hiding behind a façade to know evasion when he saw it. She'd clammed up the minute he'd mentioned the old man in the swamp. Possibly it was because of her father, but he didn't think so. If it were just the mention of those murky waters that made her think of her father, he'd expect a different reaction, like sadness. And if a mere mention of the bayou made her upset, he wouldn't expect her to offer to take him to the Villeres on the off chance he was related.

But she hadn't seemed sad. More like nervous, distracted, and frightened.

Was it because of the old man? She was definitely freaked out when they saw the creeper in the swamp. And something had set her off before that. Was it that *thing* he saw in the distance?

And what about the old man? Shay had said there were zombies in the bayou—walking dead. Julien had all but laughed it off. But could he, of all people, a man possessed by the ghost of his long dead ancestor and made to do unspeakable things, really laugh at the existence of corpses that walked the earth?

Actually, he could. First, supernatural or not, everything he'd been through could be explained by a religion, one that had been an integral part of his family for centuries. One his mother and Grandmere strongly believed in. He'd been raised in it, immersed in it, a part of it, his entire life. For all intents and purposes, it *was* his religion.

Like any religion there were aspects that, six months ago, he would have written off as superstition. Maybe his eyes had been opened to the supernatural when Sanite possessed him, but walking corpses? Even that was too farfetched for him.

With a yawn, he stretched, extending his arms far above his head and sneaking a quick peek toward Nichole's cabin. The blinds were now closed, but he could see a single candle flickering somewhere behind them. What he wouldn't give to know what she was doing in there.

The stench of rotting flesh floated in on a gust of swamp air, so potent he was forced to cover his nose. Jesus Christ, were those fish still stinking up the place? It was so bad this time his eyes watered.

Well, that was his cue. Time to hit the hay. Plucking his ass out of the chair, he flicked one last glance toward Nichole's place. Blinds still closed, candlelight still dancing behind them. At least there was tomorrow. Maybe he could get some answers from her. Not necessarily because he was nosy, but because he might be able to help.

Sanite could feel her legs moving, feel the hard ground meeting the soles of her feet over and over and over. But beyond that, she couldn't seem to feel anything else beyond cool numbness.

Even as she walked past police surrounding Laurent's sheet covered body, the red stain seeping through the white fabric did little to stir her. She had a purpose and nothing would deter her from it.

It wasn't difficult to determine the residence of the whore who had seduced her brother to his death. Standing on the front stoop, a young black maid clutched a small blond child, her pale locks falling in waves and curls rivaling her mother's now floating in the Mississippi River. Behind the maid, stood two young boys only a few years younger than Manuel—now an orphan thanks to their mother.

She walked toward the house with resolve. Everything she needed for her revenge was inside. By the time the maid noticed and tried to usher the children inside, it was too late. Stopping the door from slamming on her face, Sanite shoved her way inside.

"What are you doing?" the maid demanded, pushing the children into the other room as she tried to intercept Sanite's path. "Get out of here!"

Ignoring her, she pushed past the woman and climbed the stairs. Sanite heard the maid say a few words to the children and then footsteps on the steps behind her. She shrugged off the hand that clasped her wrist.

It was not difficult to determine the bedroom of the white whore. Bedding crumpled and pooled on the mattress, the entire room smelled of sex. With a burning that began in her belly and quickly radiated to the farthest reaches of her limbs, she realized it was the last living scent of her brother.

Yanking a brush from the vanity, she ripped hairs from the bristles and then tossed the brush aside. The noise it made when it hit the wall offered no satisfaction.

At least she had what she needed to curse that bitch. She picked up a pair of scissors laying conveniently on the vanity. Now to find the white woman's spawn...

The maid blocked her exit.

"Stand aside," Sanite said. "My quarrel isn't with you."

"I know who you are." The words were clearly accusatory.

"Then you know you should stay out of my way."

"There is nothing for you to accomplish here. You should just leave."

The maid was brave, Sanite would give her that. But that was all she would give her. *"I will. As soon as I have what I need."*

Eyes narrowed, the woman before her stood firm. "Where is my mistress? What did you do to her?"

Sanite felt the corners of her mouth raise, but felt no joy. *"Nothing she didn't deserve. She brought it on herself."*

The maid's eyes went wide with horror. "Élise did nothing to you!"

Sanite felt the rage build in her belly, felt it flood her limbs, overwhelm her mind until all she saw was red. But it was like someone else had lit the fire within. The emotion seemed removed, even as it consumed her.

Her arm coiled back and swiftly and smoothly backhanded the maid squarely across the face. Blood flew from the woman's lip as she staggered backward, slamming headfirst into the dresser and falling to the floor.

"She did everything to me! Everything!"

Her steps were heavy with anger as she searched the house. Only a couple more items and she could free herself from this place of death. The air felt diseased, and breathing it was poisoning her body and mind.

The children were huddled in a corner in the pantry. When she approached, the oldest boy stepped forward, his tiny chest puffed out like a rooster's. *"You won't hurt my brother and sister,"* he announced.

She would have liked to slit all their throats, but the girl, cowering behind her brother's back, was the same age as her Sophie. Something about that detail made Sanite pause. She would make them and their kin suffer, but she would not hurt them now. Much.

"It will only sting for a moment. Come here, boy."

He stayed back, pressing his siblings to the wall behind him.

She turned her attention to the youngest, the little blond girl Laurent had recently saved from death. "Tell me, little one, do you love your brothers?" The blond curls bobbed up and down. "Well, your mama killed my brother. And if you'd like me to spare yours, you will come here and show them how brave you can be."

Her blue eyes widened and she recoiled. Sanite held out her hand. "It'll be over soon."

The middle boy broke out in tears. His bawling only increased the fire burning through Sanite's veins. It quickly torched any patience she retained. She slapped him firmly across his wet cheek. "Enough! You're first."

Grabbing his arm, she pulled him close. "Don't move," she growled at the other children.

Using the scissors, she quickly snipped off a lock of his hair and then shoved him aside. She turned to the other boy. "Now you."

He stepped forward meekly. Using his hair as a handle, she held his head steady while she took a lock of his hair as well. The yelp he released when she pushed him behind her was strangely satisfying.

Only the girl remained. "You should have been brave," Sanite told her.

"I'm sorry," she whimpered.

"Too late."

Once Sanite had the little girl's hair, she held her wrist tight and used the scissors to slice cleanly across the small, pale forearm. She let out a high pitched wail that tore through Sanite's ears like piercing knives. Wasting no time, she smeared the dripping blood onto the locks of hair.

That was it. That was all she needed.

Sanite didn't give the children another glance. Nor did she look toward the police or her brother's body as she calmly exited the house. She had one goal and one goal only: the ritual that would complete her curse.

The slap of cool air took Nichole's breath away the second she shut the door, sending her skin into goose bump overdrive. The air conditioning was only doing its job, but the shock to the system certainly didn't help the bone deep chill she suddenly felt from her sopping wet clothes.

Bolting into the bathroom, she reached behind the door for the fluffy white robe hanging on a hook and yanked everything off her body, cursing when she heard a slight ripping sound. The drenched, clinging material made the blouse difficult to remove. Once free, she quickly swapped the clothes for the robe, wrapping herself as tightly as she could and hoping her body would warm quickly. She despised being cold.

Rubbing her palms together, she walked over to the mirror, a little surprised to see no makeup running down her face. At least she didn't *look* crazy, but her behavior tonight made her wonder if Julien thought she might be. She knew he wanted more time with her. She could practically feel his desire from that kiss.

God, that kiss. The taste of his lips, the warmth of his tongue...

She shook her head to escape the thought. Losing herself in it, in *him*, would be so easy. But she couldn't think like that right now. Daddy needed to be her number one priority. She needed answers and she was *going* to get them.

The beer buzz swimming through her head gave her courage, and minutes later she sat cross-legged on the floor in Daddy's bedroom. Except for light from the sliver of moon creeping through the sheers, the room was a shade past dark.

The moment she lit the candle, she heard the voices, their whispers and moans filling the empty space around her, making her realize just how much she tuned them out—until now. A familiar centipede-like chill crawled up her spine. The ghosts were getting closer and she was nowhere near ready. She hadn't even opened the door and they were already pressing into her head.

What was she forgetting?

Oh! Of course! Rosary beads!

Jumping up, she searched the dresser first. When that came up empty, she moved to the nightstand and then the living room. She found them in the end table drawer next to the Bible.

Returning to her position seated before the candle, she rolled the beads between her fingers. Letting her gaze soften and lose focus, she envisioned the door. More paint seemed to be missing, with huge chunks peeling like strips of black bark. She could feel the ghosts pressed against it, their presence so heavy the door appeared to bow under the weight.

"Only love, light, and peace may enter," she said softly, unease making her voice waver.

Before she could turn the knob and let them in, a violent shiver ran over her. Something moved, visible only at the farthest limits of her vision. Glancing toward the movement, she saw what looked like black, spiraling mist seep through the window cracks, dripping to the floor before swirling like a cyclone just feet from where she sat. Startled creepiness made her skin prickle. It was like having cold fingers suddenly laid against the small of her back, and a sense of dread, anger, and despair flooded her body.

She scrambled back, nearly knocking over the candle in the process. Catching it before it spilled hot wax all over the floor, she blew it out before jumping to her feet and running to the light switch. She couldn't do this. Not now.

The second light flooded the room, the mist was gone. Had she even seen it? She panned the room again, but saw nothing.

She felt the presence of something at her shoulder so strongly she spun around. Thankfully, there was no one behind her and the momentary panic she'd felt evaporated so quickly that she could almost believe it hadn't happened. Almost. Maybe she really was crazy...

At the very least, she was freaking herself out, though probably unnecessarily. Knowing she was surrounded by ghosts angry at her for ignoring them didn't help. But that was something she was used to. Knowing they were there and allowing them into her world were two different things. It was putting her on edge.

Swallowing, she forced her shoulders to relax. Maybe she should just give up before she got in over her head. She let out a sarcastic laugh. Hell, she already *was* in way over her head. This *skill* of hers had always been over her head. And she couldn't—no, wouldn't—turn her back on Daddy. The ghosts had the answers, she was sure of it. She just had to find the courage to face them and then ask. Hopefully they'd answer.

But it wasn't happening tonight.

Tomorrow. She'd try again tomorrow.

CHAPTER TEN

Julien found himself standing on Nichole's porch at two-thirty. He wasn't sure what prompted him to be so early, but there he was, waiting like an anxious puppy. Sure, he could go back to his own cabin and wait out the next thirty minutes, but he'd rather park it here and just...wait.

He hadn't seen her all day, though he had been looking. Not that he would admit it to her out loud. It was hard enough to admit to himself, but there was no denying it—he'd fallen hard and fast.

It was impossible not to. There was so much about her that was just so damn...appealing.

So when she finally emerged from the cabin, he couldn't help the schoolboy grin that surely took over his face. Her expression quickly changed that. She looked completely exhausted and her beautiful face was lined with worry.

"Everything okay?" he asked.

She just smiled and shook her head.

"We don't have to go if you don't want," he offered.

Some of the wariness faded and gratitude washed over her features. "No, I promised. It'll give me something else to focus on besides Daddy."

"Do you need any help with anything...?"

She shook her head. "I'm just prepping his estate. It's hard though, you know, since I don't think he's actually dead."

"I understand. I spent two days boxing up Grandmere's things. It was overwhelming to say the least."

"When did she die?"

"Last week."

Her mouth dropped open. "Oh my God! I'm so sorry! Here I am, wallowing in my own problems and you're freshly grieving."

"Thanks. But you don't need to apologize. She was an old woman. Blind, diabetic, and at least seventy-five pounds overweight. It was sudden and a bit shocking, but certainly not unexpected. Your father, on the other hand... that's different. Especially since..." He chewed on his words for a second. This needed to be said just right. "Especially since his disappearance is still a mystery."

"I have to find him, Julien. I have to." There was such pleading desperation and sadness in her eyes, it was all he could do not to wrap his arms around her in an attempt to bring some semblance of comfort.

"I know," he said softly. "I'll help any way I can."

Once again, gratitude made her already beautiful features stunning. "To be honest, I'm not sure what you could do, but I do appreciate the gesture." A grin spread across her full lips. "In the meantime, let's take you out to meet your long-lost toothless and possibly inbred cousins."

"I can barely contain my excitement," he said dryly.

Her grin widened. "You're in for a treat."

"I can only imagine. Wait, that reminds me. You said you were born here, right?"

"Yeah..."

"I assume you know a bit about this place then."

"Of course."

"Before we head out, can you take a look at those pictures I mentioned earlier? The one Grandmere had in her closet? Your buddy Miss Puts was no help."

"Well if she couldn't help, I doubt I can."

"Can't hurt." He pulled the pictures from his wallet and showed them to her.

With delicate fingers, she took the photos and examined them with a furrowed brow. She seemed to take in every detail before flipping them over and reading the names on the back. The furrow deepened as she studied the portraits again. Finally, her gaze lifted back to his. "And you said you found these in your grandmother's room?" She held the pictures out and he returned them to his wallet and slid it into his back pocket.

"Yes. And what's even weirder is she had shrines built to them."

"Shrines?"

"In Voodoo you build a shrine to honor the dead with gifts and offerings. It gives the spirits power."

A small grimace swept across her face but was quickly wiped away. "They do have a little of the Grisé family resemblance."

"That's even weirder. Normally shrines are built to family members. Not strangers. Especially considering my family heritage."

"And what is that? I mean, how did your family get into the Voodoo business? With the store and your tours and your grandmother's shrines..."

"We came into it honestly. I'm actually descended from one of the original French New Orleans settlers, Benoît Villere. We're not quite legit though, if you know what I mean." He winked and with a bounce of her eyebrows, she nodded her understanding.

"Voodoo was brought to New Orleans through slavery," he went on, "and Benoît's mistress, my great-great-great," he waved his hand, "you know, grandmother, was a slave of mixed descent herself. Her mother was brought from the West Indies and her father was Cherokee. She passed the religion down to her children, Benoît's illegitimate children, Sanite and Laurent Villere. Sanite was a powerful Voodoo Queen in the early nineteenth century. And well...it all just trickled down."

"That's amazing."

"So you can see why it'd be a little shocking to find shrines built to these Grisé girls. I'd never even heard the name, and I've been researching my family history for five years."

"I've never seen or heard mention of them, but I know someone who might be able to help. Think you can put off meeting your inbred cousins for a few minutes?"

"I'm sure I can contain myself long enough."

Nichole led him to large utility shed where an old man huffed and puffed while tinkering with the mower. It was actually more of a tractor, and quite possibly the largest lawn "mower" Julien had ever seen. Of course, in the Quarter, there wasn't a lot of need for much more than a bottle of weed killer.

"Wendell, should you really be messin' with that?" Nichole asked, scooping up an open bottle of water as she hustled over to the old man. "Can't Leroy or Shay handle it? You look hot as blazes."

Julien hid a small smile as he pretended to scratch his face. He loved that her accent came out when she was excited or distracted.

"There ain't no way I'm letting either one of those fools touch ol' Bessie," Wendell said, his head emerging from under the open tractor "hood." His skin bright red, he wiped the dripping sweat from his face with a dirty blue rag.

Nichole offered the bottle and he took it and a giant drink. "Thanks, darlin'." Mopping more of the sweat from his withered face, he finished the bottle and then jutted his chin toward Julien. "Who's the mulatto?"

Julien blinked. He'd heard that term spoken out loud twice in his entire life, both of them here. Nichole seemed unfazed. "Wendell, this is Julien. Julien Villere."

He offered his hand. "Of the New Orleans Villeres. Not the swamp variety I hear you have here."

"That don't surprise me. You don't look much like a man whose mama and daddy are related." He wiped the grease from his hands with the same blue rag, and then offered it to Julien.

He took the filthy rag and wiped his hands before shaking Wendell's. He was pretty sure the rag made his hands dirtier, and definitely damper, but maybe people out here bonded over shared grease.

"So what can I do for ya, NOLA Villere?" Wendell asked, stuffing the rag back into his pocket.

After verifying all the oil was off his hands, Julien produced the Grisé pictures. "I found these in my grandmother's bedroom after she passed. I was hoping you could shed a little light on them. I couldn't find either name in the historical archives."

Julien held the pictures out so Wendell could get a good look. The old man squinted, and then bent forward to get a better look, straining with each additional inch he leaned. For a millisecond his eyes widened beyond slits and then narrowed again. "Nope," he said, turning his attention back to the tractor.

"You've never seen them at all? They do bear the Grisé name..."

"That don't mean nothin'. Lots of slaves took the name after the war."

"Um... Pretty sure these women aren't slaves."

"Are you sure, Wendell?" Nichole interjected. "The portraits were taken in the foyer. I recognize the stairs."

Julien had to look at the pictures once again to see it. She was right. The ornate post of the spiraling staircase sat to the right of each woman, the carvings distinct and clearly from the manor. They were so beautiful he'd even taken a picture of them yesterday. He couldn't believe he hadn't noticed then.

"You're mistaken." Wendell had ducked his gray head back under the tractor hood, the sound of clinking tools drifting out with his gargled voice.

"But—"

"Nikki, unless you or your friend are going to help me figure out why ol' Bessie ain't startin', you'd best be on your way."

The sound of metal on metal, a thud, and then Wendell's curse, "Dammit!" filled the shed.

"Are you okay—?"

"Just get goin', Nikki. I don't have time for this."

A frown filled her entire face.

"C'mon," Julien said with a tilt of his head. "Let's leave him be."

She shook her head, the frown deepening, but still turned toward the exit.

"Thanks for your help," Julien said dryly.

Wendell just grumbled.

Outside, Nichole waited with tightly folded arms, her frown no less severe. "I don't get it," she said through tight lips.

"Miss Puts was the same way. I take it they're related?"

"Brother and sister." She stared toward the shed where Wendell was now cursing loudly. "I don't know what they're hiding."

"So you think they're hiding something?"

Her gaze swung back to him. "Definitely."

"Those were my thoughts, too."

With a sigh, she dropped her arms. "Well, I guess we can at least visit the swamp. Maybe you'll find something useful there."

"Like malaria?"

Finally a smile replaced her frown. "If you're lucky."

They traveled down the main channel for a good thirty minutes before Nichole finally slowed the boat. With the rush of the wind, splash of the water, and constant buzz of the motor, talking was impossible. Julien was happy to sit back, enjoy the breeze, and watch the scenery.

And by scenery, he didn't just mean the blur of greenery whizzing by, but Nichole. Out on the open water, she seemed much more content. With all the worry wiped from her face, she looked radiantly relaxed. And happy. Serene really. It was scenery he could see every day and not tire of it.

When they finally slowed and pulled out of the main channel onto a narrow stream choked thick with trees draped in Spanish moss, the worry came back. He could tell she tried to hide whatever was making her lips tight and her jaw tense, but the stress was written in her eyes.

"What's wrong?" he asked, elevating his voice to be heard over the low whine of the boat engine.

With a shake of her head, she offered a terse smile and nothing more.

He didn't press. At this point he knew better. But he would figure out what caused those worry lines around her dark brown eyes sooner rather than later.

He barely saw the shack even as they pulled up to a rickety wooden dock. It blended perfectly into the trees around it. Set off the water on a patch of marshy-looking grass, the gray, weathered wood siding practically disappeared into the background. On closer examination, he noticed a threadbare couch on the porch, the broken glass in the window, and a pair of shriveled up chicken feet hung on the door.

That definitely piqued his interest.

Blood splatters in the boat docked beside them caught his attention. Ropes with huge hooks attached were puddled in a corner, bits of animal flesh still clinging to the rusted barbs.

"They hunt alligators," Nichole said, her voice low.

"I suppose that should make me feel better," he replied, taking in the gruesome scene once more before turning to her.

Her expression was flat, but there was a hint of disgust tugging at the corners of her mouth. "No, it shouldn't," she said sincerely. Whatever she associated with the Villeres and hunting alligators did not make her happy.

He continued to pan the view. It was eerily quiet, without even a whisper of a breeze. Everything was perfectly still, the moss hanging like ripped up rags on a wooden clothesline. Abruptly, the smell of rotting flesh blasted his senses, its sweet putrid odor making him gag.

He coughed. "Jesus, do they ever wash this shit off?"

"It doesn't look that way."

His attention was briefly distracted by her tanned, muscular legs as she stepped out of the boat. Smooth and tight, the skin looked strokably soft. He could only imagine how they'd feel wrapped around his waist.

Coughing again, this time to clear his head instead of his throat, he climbed out of the boat and joined her on the unsteady dock. He was having a hard time keeping his focus on his own feet, and when the dock shifted under his weight, he stumbled into her.

She glanced over her shoulder as he attempted to play it cool and brush off the misstep. "Are you staring at my ass again?"

"Not anymore."

She actually smiled. Affirmation that her interest in him last night hadn't been all alcohol driven. It was a good sign.

"Don't come any closer!" a voice cracked, interrupting the moment. "This is private property! Getcher asses gone now, before my son—"

The sound of a gun being cocked echoed through the still air.

His hands shot up. "Hey, whoa, we aren't here to cause any trouble."

The screen door creaked loudly as it was pushed open. Stepping through it and onto the porch, a massive man emerged with a shotgun pointed directly at them. Shirtless, his gut hung over dirty jeans.

"You on private property," he said. "I'm gonna count to three and ya better be gone!"

Julien wondered briefly if he could actually count that high.

"One..."

"Eugene, it's me, Nichole!"

"Two..."

She looked thoroughly confused, but Julien wasn't taking any chances the threat was empty. Grabbing her hand, he spun her around and pushed her toward the boat. Keeping his body between her and the imbecile behind him, he said, "Go, I'm right behind you!"

"Three!"

The boat seemed a million miles away as they took off toward it. Behind them, a deafening shot blasted through the air, making them duck simultaneously.

"I ever see ye snooping 'round here again, I'll shoot to kill!"

Nichole reached the boat first and was already uniting the ropes when he leapt in beside her like he was a fucking track star competing in the long jump. The boat rocked violently with his hard landing.

Nichole was still fumbling with the ropes when he started the engine. He waited just long enough for slip the rope free before throwing the throttle into reverse. Once clear of the structure, he shifted gears and pushed the boat motor to its limit. The back of the boat dipped down as it fought the water's resistance.

His heart pounding violently in his chest, he tossed a quick glance over his shoulder. The dock and shack had already disappeared into the trees.

Who the hell was that crazy asshole? If he were actually related to these people, his family seemed fucking tame in comparison.

"Julien!!" Nichole shouted over the boat's roaring engine.

"I got this!"

"No, you idiot. You've been shot!"

He followed her eyes and looked down. Blood covered the sleeve of his T-shirt and was dripping down his right arm. How the fuck could he have gotten shot? He didn't even feel it.

Climbing over him, she pushed him aside and grabbed the wheel. "Sit over there and hang on," she said.

Hand cupped over his shoulder to catch the blood running down his arm, he stumbled over to the seat and fell onto it. In a daze, he watched in awe as she navigated easily through the channel. A cloud of heavy exhaust surrounded him and he could almost taste the gas fumes. That was probably why he felt so lightheaded...

Or maybe it was the blood. Lifting his hand, he glanced down at it. Red and sticky without an inch of flesh exposed. His head wobbled unsteadily on his neck. Yeah, it was probably the blood.

A towel came out of nowhere, hitting him in the face. "Hold that against the wound and press hard," she shouted. "You're bleeding like a bitch."

Feeling about as masculine as a kitten, he nodded, doing his best to keep his head intact and the contents of his stomach where they belonged. Obeying her command, he pressed the towel against the wound, wincing. That fucker hurt. Unlike blood, pain was something he could handle. He just hoped like hell he wouldn't pass out.

CHAPTER ELEVEN

The ride back to the plantation seemed to take hours instead of minutes. Every time Nichole glanced over at Julien all she could see was blood. There was so much of it, even the towel she'd given him was stained with crimson. The first thing she needed to do was get him to the hospital. Though a little pale, judging by the way he made lighthearted jokes at every opportunity, he didn't seem nearly as scared as she.

She didn't ease up on the throttle until they were practically on top of the dock. Their abrupt stop sent a wave of water over the planks. Julien tossed out the bumper nearest to him, but momentum still made the boat hit the wood with a thud. Quickly looping the ropes over the dock cleat, she wasted only a few seconds securing the boat before jumping out onto the platform.

Boat still swaying, Julien stood carefully.

She offered her hand. "Here," she said. "Let me help you."

He actually looked a little insulted, glancing at her hand and then at her. "I think I've got this." He stepped from the boat unassisted, but he still seemed a little unsteady.

"Can you walk? I won't be able to bring my car down here, but if you can make it to the cabins, I can run and grab it."

He stared at her. "What are you talking about? Of course I can walk."

"Are you kidding? We've got to get you to a doctor!"

Still pressing the towel to his wound, he held up his free hand. "Unnecessary. I'm fine."

She couldn't believe how nonchalant he was, especially with blood splattered all over his shirt. "You're not fine, Julien, you've been shot for Christ's sake!"

"It's just a flesh wound," he said, grinning like he was enjoying some inside joke.

"You're freaking crazy!"

"No, really." He removed the towel, showing that the bleeding had mostly stopped. There was a divot of missing flesh, though, pink and raw and still seeping.

"I think the loss of blood has made you loopy, and secondly—"

"No *secondly*. I'm fine and I'm definitely not going to a hospital. I'll bandage it up myself if I have to."

"Holy crap, you are a piece of work! And you're effing stubborn." Her head felt like someone had stuck it in the oven. Frustration was going to make it explode if she didn't calm down.

"Good," he said with a wink. "I'm glad we can agree on something."

The wink did nothing for her disposition. "Argh! I could throttle you!"

"Not usually what I'm into, but I think I can make an except for you."

She rolled her eyes. "C'mon. Let me at least get you cleaned up. Daddy has an extensive first aid kit at home."

Marching toward the cottage, she didn't bother to see if he followed. She could hear him behind her and that was good enough. If she had to look at smug face, no matter how handsome, she was going to go back to the Villeres', get the gun, and kill him herself.

God, had they really been shot at? It seemed so surreal.

Chills crawled over her skin at the thought of Julien's quick decision to shove her out of the way. She hadn't thought about it at the time, of course, but his reaction quite possibly saved her life. If he hadn't stepped in (literally), she would have continued to stand there like an idiot while Two-Tooth shot her.

As soon as they reached the cabin, she instructed him to take a seat at the kitchen table. "Stay put and keep holdin' that towel firmly until I get back."

"Yes, ma'am," he returned with a Cheshire grin.

She could have slapped that grin right off his face. Setting her jaw, she escaped into the bathroom to gather the first aid kit.

Why was she so angry? Was it because he was refusing medical care? Because he took control? Because he protected her? Because she was worried about him?

God, all of the above.

With a sigh, she grabbed the kit and jogged back to the kitchen.

Shirt off, Julien had his feet propped on the chair next to him like it was just another Thursday afternoon and he was taking a load off. He still had the towel pressed to his shoulder, but that wasn't where her gaze went. The wet shirt from the night before might have hinted at his fabulous physique, but it could compare with the bare version, glistening with moisture from recently being rinsed. The smooth, taut, damp skin emphasized every hard ridge, dip, and valley of muscle.

Taking a deep breath, she forced herself to refocus.

"I still think I should take you to the hospital," she said again, placing the medical supplies on the table.

"You worry too much. I'm fine, remember? Flesh wound." There was that cocky smile again.

She scooted a chair next to him and reached for the peroxide. "This might sting a little."

She lightly dabbed the liquid on the raw skin. He hissed as his breath sucked in.

"Sorry. That was the worst part." She blew on the wound.

His eyes were locked on her when she glanced up at him. There was no denying the lust pooling in them. She swallowed against the heat it generated within her.

What was wrong with her? The man had been shot and she was completely turned on.

Blinking, she returned to disinfecting the wound. Once she got a really good look, she found the injury was roughly the size of a penny and fairly superficial. He was right—a doctor was probably unnecessary. Blood had a way of scaring people...especially when an injury bled as heavily this one did. Relief didn't begin to cover how she felt. As hard as it was to admit, the fact was, she was beginning to really like him.

"I think we should at least call the police," she said, gathering up bandages.

"Nah, we were on private property. They kind of had every right..."

"Every right to shoot you?" Her voice shot up an octave.

"Hey, I'm not happy about it either, but nothing good can come from me filing a complaint on those crazy bastards. They could have shot us both, tossed our dead bodies in the swamp...and probably gotten away with it."

"You keep doing nothing and they might." She could feel her blood pressure rising again.

With fingers that weren't quite as careful as they should have been, she placed a piece of gauze over the wound and taped it down.

"Let it go, Nichole," he said, lifting his feet from the chair and standing up. "Whoa." Stumbling, he placed a hand on the table to steady himself. "I must have gotten up too fast."

She shot up out of her chair and grabbed his injured arm. He winced.

"Oh! Sorry!"

"I'm beginning to wonder whether you're trying to help me or hurt me," he teased.

"You need to sit back down and drink something. The blood loss is making you lightheaded. Here." She pulled gently on his arm, guiding him toward the sofa.

"I could use a cold one," he said as he sat.

"You need orange juice, not beer."

"At least put a little vodka in it."

This game of his stubbornness versus hers was making her crazy. When she plopped orange juice and an Oreo cookie on the end table beside him, he laughed.

"Thanks, Mom."

"Hilarious...just drink it."

"Girl, you need to relax. Come here." His outstretched hand reached for her.

She knew right then how much she wanted him. True, he drove her crazy, but apparently in all the good ways as well as the bad.

Against her better judgment, she did what he asked and took his hand. He pulled her onto the couch beside him, and then, much to her disappointment, released his hold on her.

"I feel like I should get you some ibuprofen or something."

"In a second. But first, thanks for, well...this." He gestured toward his bandaged bare shoulder.

"Anytime."

"I get shot? I'll keep that in mind."

With a chortle, she let her head fall back wearily onto the couch. "God, can you believe that? I don't know what got into Two-Tooth. I mean, he's always been weird, but shooting at us..."

"Two-Tooth?"

Her head flopped to the side to look at him. "Eugene Villere—your long-lost cousin."

His full lips twisted into a grimace. "Nice."

"You could almost be twins," she said, fighting the urge to smile and forcing her face to reveal as little as possible.

"Hey, teasing is *my* thing."

"Nope. You don't get to call dibs on flirting."

"So you *are* flirting with me." His voice low and thick; the lust back in his eyes made the green sparkle.

Uh-oh.

The muscles of his abs popped as he leaned toward her, and she had this strong desire to dance her fingers over them. Wetting her lips, she swallowed.

"I can, um, get you one of Daddy's shirts. I think yours is ruined."

"I'm good."

Yes. Yes, he was.

She swallowed again.

He lightly traced her bare arm, leaving a trail of goosebumps in the wake, pausing when he reached her neck to brush the hair from her shoulders. She closed her eyes as his lips pressed against her neck.

"I love the smell of your perfume," he murmured into her flesh.

A response was trapped in the back of her throat as his kisses continued up her neck and landed on her ear. He cupped the side of her jaw and turned her face to him, tracing her jawline ever so gently, guiding her until their lips met. His soft, warm touch felt just as amazing as the first time they kissed, only better and more tender somehow. Goosebumps rippled over her, joining the ones lingering on her arm, and heat tore through her body, reminding her how incredibly sexy she found him.

A wisp of cool air breezed through her hair, awakening her senses.

"Have you forgotten about your daddy?"

Her eyes flashed open and she jerked back, breaking off the kiss and panning the room. She could've sworn that voice whispered in her ear.

His eyes followed hers as they darted around. "What's wrong?"

"Nothing," she replied automatically. It definitely wasn't nothing, though. Every hair on the back of her neck stood at attention, and that usually meant one thing.

It had been years since the ghosts randomly broke through her barriers. Years of practice had made them strong. The attempts at contact must be weakening the wall. She mentally reinforced the barriers and then turned to Julien with what she hoped wasn't a feeble smile.

"I just thought I heard someone outside," she said. "I'm sure it was just the wind."

He looked far from convinced. Unfortunately, it didn't matter. However the ghosts had broken through, what they accused her of was true. Of course she hadn't forgotten Daddy, but she wasn't any closer to finding him either.

She had to make another attempt again. If they were accusing her of forgetting Daddy, they must know more about what happened to him.

"Nichole?"

Julien was eyeing her carefully, and she realized she was perched on the edge of the couch, shoulders bunched up with tight tension. When his hand pressed against the small of her back, she nearly jumped off the couch. She tried, and promptly failed, to relax.

Okay, this wasn't going to work. She rose.

"You know, it's getting late, and it's been a really long day. You should probably get some rest."

Julien's hand, still floating from where it rested against her back, fell to the couch. "Okay…"

She hated the look in his eyes. Disappointment, confusion, wariness.

Even if she wanted to, she couldn't explain any of this. He'd think she was crazy—just like everyone else.

"Your daddy needs you."

The voice made her visibly startle. How was the woman getting through? She'd strengthened the barrier…

She paced to the kitchen and grabbed Julien's bloody shirt. How the spirit was getting through didn't matter. She obviously wanted something, pulling at Nichole like an unsatisfied itch. And if the woman had answers, she couldn't waste any more time. Julien had to go, and fast.

He was standing by the couch when she returned. His body looked even better erect. She immediately shot her gaze to the floor.

"Here's your shirt," she said, holding out the bloody bundle of fabric.

He lifted it from her hands. "Probably going to have to let this one go."

"Yeah... Okay, well, try to get some rest."

"Nichole." His fingers wrapped around her arm, their gentle grasp keeping her from running away.

Her gaze flicked to him for about two seconds before she had to look away. Those eyes...they just looked so confused and...hurt.

"Sorry, I, um, I just have something to do."

He dropped his hand and then rubbed his face. "Okay, of course. I guess it *is* getting late."

She avoiding making eye contact as they walked to the door, keeping her gaze averted as she opened the door. She didn't dare look at him even as he stepped onto the porch. Seeing that hurt again in his eyes might just break her resolve.

"Take care of your arm," she said. "Goodnight." The door closed on him before he could react.

CHAPTER TWELVE

Once again, Julien found himself standing on his cottage porch staring befuddled in the direction of Nichole's place, only this time half-naked and clutching a bloody shirt. He realized she was under a lot of stress, but the switch in her moods was leaving him reeling.

And in need of a cold shower.

Or the very least a drink.

He'd left the bottle of Beam on the porch, sitting innocently on the small end table tucked between the two faux wicker chairs. Twisting off the cap, he took a long, healthy drink. The sting of the liquor sliding down his throat was almost as sharp as the stinging of his war wound.

Shot by a gun. Holy fuck.

A crazy afternoon turned into a crazy evening. This place sure had its share of demons. And he thought his family home was bad. What other secrets did Plantation Grisé hold? He'd bet his last dollar there were plenty.

He took another swig of bourbon. He'd give Nichole her moment, but that was it. He only had so much patience. It was time he confront her issues. There was no denying her attraction to him at this point. Something else had her spooked, and he wanted to help her. Not just because helping her might end this hot and cold game she was playing, but he genuinely wanted to assist. With all the fucked up shit he'd experienced, he was sure he could offer something.

His stomach grumbled angrily and he realized he hadn't eaten in hours. And neither had Nichole. Bringing her dinner would give him the perfect excuse to knock on her door without looking like a complete tool. Besides, the girl needed to eat. Hell, maybe low blood sugar was behind her change in mood.

Not likely, but food was in order anyway. He'd give her a few minutes to do whatever she needed to do, and in the meantime, he'd run up to the main house and score some grub. After he took a shower and put on some fresh clothes, of course. Otherwise the hotel guests were likely to think him some crazed murderer. The police in this bayou had proven incompetent, last thing he needed was them breathing down his neck.

It took everything Nichole had to shut the door on Julien. Eyes closed, she leaned against the door, her trembling hand still wrapped around the cool metal knob.

God, the look on his face. She couldn't believe how important he'd become to her in such a short time. The things they had already experienced together were definitely bonding. And he was proving to be the kind of man she needed. One that didn't balk at a challenge, who seemed to put up with her quirks, who really seemed to get her... It also helped that he was considerate, chivalrous, and amazing to look at.

Of course, how long would he put up with her pushing him away? Maybe she should just suck it up and tell him the whole truth. Maybe she should do it before she attempted to open the door to the ghost world again. How wonderful it would be to have someone to talk to, someone she could trust.

She started to turn the knob to call Julien back when the woman's voice interrupted her. *"Your daddy needs you. Don't let him down."*

Her hand fell.

Guilt nearly floored her. She'd already indulged a little too much in the pleasure that was Julien Villere. She couldn't keep avoiding her responsibilities.

Filled with dread but determined to succeed, she made her way to the bedroom, keeping her gaze focused on the chest of drawers holding the items she needed, like if she looked away for two seconds she'd never be able to complete her task. Rosary beads draped around it, the candle sat on the center of the dresser, blackened wick contrasting against the bright white wax. The open book of matches lay beside it, missing stubs of twisted out matches a reminder of the two failed attempts she'd already made. She could hear the mocking chicken clucks even as she retrieved the items and set them on the floor.

Lingering at the edge of her thoughts, the mysterious spirit's voice played over and over in her mind. *"I can help you find your daddy..."* she promised.

A swirling of whisperings crept in behind the voice, twisting in endless white noise in the background of her mind. She couldn't seem to shut any of it out and she knew her protective barriers were weakening.

It didn't matter. She had to try. If she could just find the strength, she could keep them at bay. But they were like the buzzing of cicadas in the middle of summer. So loud it became difficult to think.

Or remember her grandmother's words: *"Show them who's boss, Nikki. You can't hesitate for even a second, or they'll walk all over you. You have to always stay in control."*

Stay in control. Easier said than done. It didn't matter how hard she tried, they seemed hell-bent to break through whatever shield she tried to put up.

The heels of her palms blackened her vision in a desperate attempt to clear her thoughts and remember everything she had done before, what she might have forgotten. Voices, moans, and whispers called her name. They were everywhere.

Before she dared light the candle, before she even envisioned the door, she had to try to piece together her last attempts at contact and why they might have failed. She pushed her brows tightly, as if doing so would help remember.

"Candles.
Rosary.
And.
And...?"
Of course! How could she be so careless?

Salt. That's what she'd been missing. Jumping to her feet, she dashed to the kitchen, grabbed the blue box in the cabinet, and then sprinted back to the bedroom. Plopping back onto the floor, she pulled out the metal port and carefully poured the white crystals. Encircling herself with a thin line of the salt's protection was the one thing she hadn't completed the first two times.

Hopefully, it was the link she'd been missing.

"Breathe, Nichole," she whispered to herself. "Just concentrate on breathing."

Her hand trembled as she struck the first match, shaking so much the flame promptly went out. It took a second match, then a third, then a fourth before she was finally able to light the candle.

After a few deep breaths as Gran had instructed so many years ago, followed a quick inventory to verify every step had been finally been executed correctly, she looped the rosary around her neck. Clasping the smooth beads between her fingers, she bowed, at the same time envisioning the same peeling black door separating her from the ghost world. She may have neglected the salt, but she'd also been so impatient to connect with Daddy she'd neglected her Father.

"Holy Father, please guide and protect me as I invite the surrounding souls to communicate."

Something like an electric shock ran right though her. Gasping, she jerked backward, like somebody had punched her in the chest. For a moment, she was disoriented. As she righted herself, a breathless noise that seemed to be trying to mimic a scream shot from her lungs. Her skin jumped in the strangest way, like a horse's does when a horsefly bites it.

And then everything went still. No buzzing, no whispering from ghosts in the background of her mind, no obnoxious horseflies.

Silence. Nothing but silence...

She startled when her ears popped and the pressure in the room changed.

Pop, pop, pop...

Loud whispers engulfed her like a swirling swarm of angry bees swarming around her body, waiting for the perfect time to sting. She fumbled for a moment, wondering what she should do, and steadied herself against the strange currents in the room.

Somehow, Gran's voice peaked above the rest. *"They can smell your fear, child."*

She looked down at her trembling hands, momentarily fixated on their constant quivering. She wanted to run away. Wanted to run straight to Julien's arms.

No. She wouldn't give up this time. And she couldn't give in to temptation. Even if that temptation was Julien Villere.

Suddenly the peeling black door burst open and the whirling of whispers increased until what sounded like the voices of hundreds of people pulverized her ears. Like headphones that hadn't been properly turned down before the play button was pressed.

With a scream, her hands slammed to the sides of her head, as if doing so would somehow bring the volume down. Clamping her eyes tightly shut, she tried to regain control, tried to mentally restrain them. It wasn't working.

The ghosts were quickly overwhelming her. Their presence increased all around her until she felt like she was trapped in an overfull elevator. They pushed and shoved against her, demanding answers, demanding attention. Their questions flooded her ears. How did they die? Where were their families? Why were they there? More and more questions until their voices became a din of barely distinguishable words.

She wanted to slam the door on them, but if she wanted answers about Daddy, she had to face them. Carefully she cracked open an eye and immediately wished she hadn't. They were everywhere, pushing and shoving, mouths on hollowed faces working overtime as they bombarded her with questions. Letting out a deep breath, she pressed her shaking hands to the floor and stood.

Now is your chance. Ask them about Daddy.

The thought seemed to enrage them. Electricity buzzed through the air and she could feel their anticipation building.

Pop. Pop. Pop, pop, pop, pop!

The swarm of angry bees engulfed her and she realized there was no need to ask. They could already read her thoughts the same way she could hear theirs. The telepathy was a two-way street. They already knew she wanted answers about Daddy. And she could tell it didn't matter. At least not right now. They weren't there to give answers, only get them.

But she didn't have answers to give. And if she didn't sever the contact and shut out the din of their inquiries, she was going to lose her ever-loving mind.

Closing her eyes, she brought back the door the same way Gran had taught her so many years ago. The ghosts fought back, but using the force of her mind, she pushed them through one by one. Gripping the rosary tight, she prayed. With their constant thoughts flooding her mind, concentration was almost impossible. Beads of sweat covered her face from the effort, dripping from her nose and down her neck. Her fingers were raw from her hold on the rosary and her shirt was drenched, but finally, she forced them all behind the door and carefully locked it.

Lifting her head, she opened her eyes. Thankfully, all of the ghosts that had been standing in the room were gone, but the thick air still held vibrations of them. She was able to enjoy a brief moment of silence before another loud pop exploded in the air, and the voices, the terrible and overwhelmingly intrusive voices, shot back into her head, lingering like a bleeding wound.

She tried again, and again, and again to shove them behind the door. She begged them to stop. She blew out the candle and prayed harder. Nothing worked. Nothing would silence them.

Sweat was no longer the only thing wetting her face. Tears streamed down her cheeks.

Since the salt she'd encircled herself with didn't seem to be working, she stepped over it and walked into the kitchen with the hope leaving the room would help. That perhaps the ghosts were tied to the bedroom since they'd been summoned there.

It didn't help. Stabbing pain formed beneath her brow bone, like the ghosts in her head were crowding her brain. Retrieving some ibuprofen and a glass from the cabinet, she fumbled with the faucet, her hands still trembling violently, shaking so much she could barely hold onto the cup.

Dropping the glass into the sink with a thud, she leaned heavily on the counter. The voices seemed to be getting louder, like they were shouting to be heard. She tried to block them again, but nothing happened. She had to make them stop. There was no way she could continue like this.

Movement seemed to help a little, if only to distract her momentarily. Maybe if she kept her body moving, she could think. Maybe even figure out what to do.

If not, she'd go crazy trying.

The kitchen was a zoo, and nearly two hours later, Julien walked back down the dark path to the cottages carrying Styrofoam boxes crammed full of Étoufée and jambalaya. It was another pitch black night, the moon nowhere to be seen. Unlike his mother, Julien didn't pay attention to the lunar cycles, so he had no idea if this was a new moon or if it was simply hiding behind a cloud. He did know it was dark as fuck. If he was lucky, he wouldn't break his neck tripping over his own feet.

When he paused at his porch to grab the bourbon, he was once again hit with the overwhelming stench of decay. It was so bad he had to shove his nose into the crook of his elbow.

"Jesus! Fuck!"

How on earth could those damn fish still be stinking up the place? And why was the smell even drifting up this way? There wasn't any fucking wind... And why was he only smelling them at night? It didn't add up.

Unless it was something else.

That might make sense, except it didn't reek like death before he left to get food. A dead animal under the porch or something could be the cause, but for said dead thing to stink bomb the place after only an hour? Dead shit didn't suddenly decide to start stinking. It usually worked its way up to full blown stank.

It was like some rotting corpse was just out for a stroll.

There was that whole *zombie* rumor...

More than likely, one of the dogs he'd seen roaming the plantation had found a carcass and brought it up from the swamp. No matter. As disgusting as it smelled, he had to find the source. The stench would totally put a damper on dinner. Hell, *his* appetite was quickly exiting the building.

Setting the food and Beam on the end table, he briefly glanced toward Nichole's cabin. Candle light once again flickered behind closed shades. She sure liked her candles. Maybe she was having a Calgon moment or something. That would be good. She definitely needed to relax.

The stench was easy to trace. He didn't even need to try it was that potent. For a brief moment, he attempted to sniff the air like a bloodhound, but that just made him gag. Covering his nose, he let his watering eyes lead the way.

Toward Nichole's cabin. Toward the swamp.

The nonexistent moonlight didn't begin to penetrate the darkness between the edge of the old slave quarters and the hundred feet of open grassland before swamp and trees took over. The smell was definitely stronger over there.

Treading carefully, nose still shoved into the crook of his elbow, Julien crept down the modest incline toward the tree line. By the time he was twenty feet away, the stench was overwhelming. It was nothing like death he'd smelled over the years. Living in the Quarter in a house from the 1800s, he'd certainly smelled his share of dead animals. Mostly rodents, but still.

This was sickly sweet. Pungent in a way he couldn't begin to describe. And so fucking strong. It had to be a goddamn elephant or something.

A flash of eyes caught his, briefly set off by scarce light hundreds of feet away. He turned to it, jumping a little when whatever animal the eyes belonged to scampered away. A stick snapped behind him and he spun, nearly running into...it.

What used to be a man stood before him. Flesh dripped from a skeletal face, hanging in drooping gray slabs like rotten roast beef. Pieces of skull were exposed, shining dully through the exposed flesh. One eye socket was an empty, gaping black hole. The other eye was milky white and drooped from the socket. Tattered shards of filthy fabric hung from the monster's limbs, the remnants of clothing from years past. He caught of glimpse of velvet and brocade among exposed bones and more dripping gray flesh.

A silent scream caught in his throat as the corpse reached for him, what used to be a mouth working up and down, hinged only on one side of its jaw. It moved clumsily and slowly, and stood at least a foot away, but Julien still jumped backward on legs made of springs. He turned and bolted back toward the cabins. When a root took out his feet, he merely somersaulted over his right shoulder, jumped back up, and kept running. He didn't pause, hesitate, or look back. He *definitely* didn't look back.

And he was pretty sure he didn't breathe until the door to Nichole's cabin slammed closed behind him.

CHAPTER THIRTEEN

Wide-eyed and a ghastly shade of gray, Nichole was doing laps around the kitchen, wringing her hand so rapidly and with such force they were a stark combination of red and white.

She didn't seem to notice him come in. Leaning against the door, panting with enough force to blow the pig's brick house down, he wasn't exactly quiet. Yet she continued to stare at the floor, her expression pained as she paced like a madwoman.

He said her name. If she heard him, he couldn't tell. Her brows did push together as her eyes clamped shut. Cupping her hands over her ears, he saw her mouth moving. It looked like she was saying, "Shut up, shut up, shut up."

She wasn't talking to him, he was sure of it.

Something else was going on.

"Nichole?"

Eyes still clenched shut, she visibly winced. After taking a deep breath to try and calm his still rapidly beating heart, Julien pushed away from the doorway and walked carefully toward her. She paced her way into the bedroom and he tentatively followed, repeating her name.

Again, she didn't respond, instead flopping onto the bed and curling into a ball, pressing fingers into her ears.

And suddenly he knew why. It was the salt circle that gave it away, and the recently lit candle sitting in the center. This was a scene he'd witnessed before. Many times, when his mother had an...episode.

Everything became crystal clear.

Why Nichole knew her father wasn't dead.

Why she seemed so secretive and guarded.

She was a medium. Like his mother. Like Grandmere. The salt was to protect her from the ghosts when she summoned them, to keep them at arm's length.

Something had obviously gone wrong.

Jumping to her feet, she breezed past him and back into the kitchen. He caught up to her as she leaned against the counter, her body rocking back and forth. With gentle hands, he took her shoulders and turned her to him. Only then did she actually look at him.

And immediately burst into tears.

He took her into his arms. "It's okay," he said, stroking her back with velvet hands. "It's okay."

"No, it isn't. I can't—I can't—" She shook her head into his chest. "They won't stop talking. They're in my head and they won't stop..." Sniffing loudly, she shook her head again and pulled back, wiping furiously at her eyes.

"I'm f-fine," she said, a waver in her voice. "I just..." She sniffed again, took a deep breath, and then squared her shoulders. "You should go." She pulled away completely, the tips of her fingers massaging her temples as she walked away.

"I don't think so." He took her arm and turned her back to him, lifting her chin so she had to look at him. "I can help you. Let me help you."

Brows deeply furrowed, her head moved rapidly from side to side.

"I can," he insisted.

Tears once again brimmed her eyes. He reached for her and she jerked back.

"I'm sorry. I just—" She paused, once again shaking her head furiously. "You can't help me. The only person who could help me has been dead for years."

"Do you have any booze in this house?"

She stared at him incredulously, her expression clearly saying, "What the fuck?"

"Not for me." Retrieving his wallet, he pulled out the baggie containing the small amount of pills he kept tucked away for emergencies. "Valium," he told her.

She looked both reserved and hopeful. "I don't know..." She stared at the pills like they might just be the cure to an incurable disease. Suddenly her eyes lifted to his. "Why do you have Valium?"

"I'll explain everything later. Trust me, one of these babies and a shot of whiskey, or any other booze, and you'll be out."

Her hand rubbed across her eyes wearily. And then with a grimace, she said, "I am tired."

"I know." Pulling out one of the kitchen table chairs, he helped her into it. Once seated, her elbows landed heavily on the table and she sank into her hands, pressing so firmly into her temples until the skin was white around her fingers. With tiny movements, her body once again rocked back and forth.

"Booze?" he pressed. He had plenty of alcohol in his own cabin—the bottle on the porch and the others still in his pack. He could run and grab the Beam, but not only was there a corpse walking around out there, he didn't want to leave her alone.

He did have an idea how to help her besides just letting her sleep for a few hours, something that had helped his mother. Eventually, he would be forced to leave her in order to retrieve the items he needed, but he wasn't going until he knew she was out—and safe.

Without lifting her eyes from the table, she gestured toward one of the cabinets. On the very top shelf sat a few dusty bottles. Grabbing a slightly less dusty bottle of whiskey, he poured a shot, and then handed her a pill and the glass.

She pursed her lips before tossing the pill into her mouth, followed by the liquor, making a face as she wiped her mouth with the back of her hand.

He sat beside her, gently resting his hand on her back. She didn't fight this time, but the rocking did intensify, along with the pained expression.

"Just give it a minute," he soothed.

As soon as she was asleep, he'd gather the items he needed. She had a white candle already, so he just needed a base (a couple sticks from the swamp would do), some fabric, a little Spanish moss for stuffing, and a lock of her hair. The vial for salt could prove a little difficult, but he might have something in his bag...

Finally, after about fifteen minutes, the rocking subsided. She turned to him with half-lidded eyes.

"Told you," he said with a smile.

Scooping her up, he carried her to the bedroom and placed her gently on the mattress. He sat beside her, continuing to stroke her back and hair until her body completely stilled and her breathing deepened.

When he confirmed she was asleep, he rose and headed for the front door. Hand on the knob, he paused, remembering the horror waiting for him outside.

What the hell was that thing? A walking corpse? A fucking zombie?

Shay wasn't joking around. There were goddamn zombies hanging out around the swamp. No wonder Nichole always seemed so freaked out when they ventured into those murky waters.

He glanced back toward the bedroom. If it wasn't for that beauty slumbering away in a drug-induced coma, there was no way he'd go out there. But she needed him, and the shit he needed was outside.

With a deep breath and a shake of his shoulders to ward off the huge case of chills running down his spine, he twisted the knob and cracked the door. Leading with his nose, he took a whiff.

The bile jumping to his throat said it was still out there. Where, he couldn't tell, but that stench was undeniable.

"Fuck, fuck, fuck, fuck."

Shit, he could use one of those Valiums now too.

He cracked his neck in each direction, set his jaw with a grunt, and yanked open the door.

"You cannot keep your daddy waiting!"

The shrill, demanding voice of a woman startled her awake. Blinking her eyes, she clumsily looked around the room while trying to clear the heavy fog of sleep. Her head felt like it had been stuffed with cotton and knives.

The room was black as tar and she lay frozen for a moment, her gut churning with sharp needles. A cool breeze slid along her arm and up the side of her face, making the fine hairs rise along her neck.

"He needs you. Now."

Her head lurched as she sat up. Chaos instantly surrounded her, growing thick with an oppressive weight against her chest. The voices returned, stirring in her mind, murmuring and whispering like they were merely waiting for the perfect second to increase in volume. Like they were toying with her.

Where was Julien? He'd put her to bed, right? Given her Valium and a shot of whiskey? That potent combo must be why her head felt so…thick.

She called his name, screaming to be heard over the voices only present in her mind. There was no response.

The thought of having to endure another second of the head-pounding madness sent her straight into panic mode, and she strained her exhausted brain to think of something, *anything* to help her before the hell she knew was coming broke loose.

Lying in this bed in the dark definitely wasn't going to cut it. Shoving the covers aside, she rose and flipped on the light. Surely there was some task that could take her mind off the roar of voices screaming between her ears.

Of course! There were a million mundane tasks requiring her attention. Like it or not, she was supposed to be organizing Daddy's estate. She might be hell-bent on finding him and confident the task was unnecessary, but regardless, it wasn't like the house couldn't use a good spring cleaning.

She went to the linen closet first. The towels and sheets were in complete disarray. Nichole started on the most tedious of tasks: the fitted bed sheet. Beginning at the top, she meticulously lined up each end and stretched them from corner to corner, wrapping and folding as she went until the sheet became a perfect square.

She was right, it *did* seem better. The voices were never completely gone, but keeping them down to a quiet shout was better than nothing. And she was willing to do almost anything.

Yanking a flat sheet off of the shelf and out of its wadded ball, she plugged in the iron and proceeded to iron the sheet into smooth perfection. And she didn't stop there. Every sheet, every towel that didn't have huge holes or stains and could be salvaged, was ironed to crisp flatness.

She busied herself for what seemed like hours, but when she glanced at the clock, her heart sank when she saw it had only been an hour. How much longer could she do this?

Pools of water blurred her vision as she felt the sting of tears; her head began pounding like a jackhammer. She wiped away the tears and went back to work.

As long as it took. That's how long.

She finished stacking and tucking and ironing the last of Daddy's linens. The shelves looked like a *Better Homes and Garden* layout. Complete perfection.

It wasn't enough. Just that small deviation in concentration and the voices increased in volume, their individual words becoming clearer. The longer she lingered between tasks, the louder they became.

She pressed her fingertips to her temples. Maybe if she pushed hard enough they would be forced out.

If the pain stabbing the inside of her skull didn't do her in, fatigue would. Sleep—or being knocked unconscious—sounded like heaven. But she was afraid if she allowed her eyes to close for even a moment, they would push through the rest of her weakened barrier and she'd be lost forever.

At this point, she was certain they'd never give up. So many lost souls angrily pushing, shouting, and screaming their way to the front of the line just to get a word in. They were desperate, but so was she...and they knew it.

Tripping over her own feet on the way to the kitchen, she struggled to open the coffee can. The tricky little filter proved even more difficult, but it wasn't long before an extra strong pot brewed.

While the coffee percolated, she scrubbed down the counters. Normally, she took cream and sugar in her coffee, but adding the ingredients seemed like they would only dilute it and prolong the caffeine intake. And that was not an option. Neither was sitting.

The scrubbing didn't stop at the counters. She removed everything from the cabinets and organized, wiped down, straightened, and damn near spit-shined the insides, outsides, and all of the contents.

The living room came next. Pausing only to crank up the air conditioner, she worked until her fingers were raw. And then she moved on to Daddy's bedroom.

Time dragged on. The voices pushed on.

And on.

And on.

And on.

Finally, when her body said, "Enough!" she collapsed against the bedroom wall, thighs trembling as she sank to the floor. Seemingly overjoyed at her lapse in concentration, the voices rose to mind-shattering shrills.

Shoving her ragged fingers into her ears, she pressed until the pain made her wince. With each push, she could hear the twisting sounds of her own flesh closing tightly, but she needed to hear something, anything but them. She even made a noise to test her own hearing. Or sanity. She wasn't sure which.

Though faint, at least she could hear her own voice, but it was only enough to know she was still alive. At this point she was beginning to wish she wasn't.

She allowed the stinging tears to fall down her cheeks as she pulled her legs up to her chest and wrapped her arms tightly around her body. It was too much. Too much.

CHAPTER FOURTEEN

Julien had never moved so fast in his life. He sprinted off Nichole's porch with Flash speed and dashed toward the nearest tree, scooping up a couple sticks and jumping to pull down some Spanish moss from a low hanging branch before bounding like a spooked horse back to his own cabin, pausing for a half a millisecond to grab the food from the porch table. Sleeping Beauty would surely be hungry after all this was resolved—assuming he *could* resolve it.

Once he'd made it safely inside and stashed the food in the fridge, he quickly went to work. The first part of his task had been relatively easy once he located a first aid kit in the bathroom medicine cabinet. It wasn't nearly as extensive as the one Nichole's father stocked, but as luck would have it, contained an "emergency" sewing kit.

After breaking the sticks into six-inch segments, he quickly lashed them together into the shape of a cross, using the lace from one of his running shoes (shoes he'd brought in case he got the urge to run—for exercise, not from zombies). He then sewed a crude body together with torn pieces of one of his T-shirts, and stuffed it with Spanish moss. A cork became the head, a Sharpie made the face. His luck held when he dug out a white-tipped push pin from the sewing kit.

But that's where his luck ran out. Having the doll made from so many personal things, and from items close to Nichole and her family in the case of the moss and sticks, should give it power, but he was afraid it wouldn't be enough. He needed a vial, something to hold salt that Nichole could wear around her neck. The other shoelace from his sneakers could secure it. All he needed was a vial…

So there he was, rummaging through the cabin like a burglar looking for loose change. At the shop back in New Orleans, they had hundreds of them. They were pre-hung on cords and often filled with essential oils or healing herbs or gimmicky potions. He could perfectly picture the box filled with empties sitting in the store room. Imported from China, they cost all of five cents apiece. He'd gladly pay fifty dollars for one now.

He'd been sure one or two might have made their way into his bag, but that wasn't the case. So then he took to scouring the cabin, hoping, praying, that he'd find a substitution. He'd been so lucky with the first aid kit, he thought he'd surely find something.

Nothing. And two hours later, sweating like a pig, he was still looking. Frustrated and ready to get in the car and speed home to get what he needed, he made his way to the kitchen to grab a glass of water. He downed two without taking a breath, and then refilled the glass and leaned against the counter.

Jesus, all he needed was a damn container he could fill with salt. He had an extra shoelace, for fuck's sake. A pill container would work, except he hadn't brought one of those either. Instead he'd shoved his "quit freaking out" pills in a damn baggie.

Wait...

He dug the crumpled bag from his pocket. Of course! It wouldn't be pretty, but that didn't matter.

Since he'd already ransacked the kitchen, he knew exactly where the salt was. He'd even set it on the counter so he could easily locate it later.

Both nervous and excited, his hands trembled as he held open the sandwich baggie and dumped the contents of the entire salt shaker inside, knowing how every grain of salt was precious—and powerful.

Please say there isn't a hole. Please say there isn't a hole.

There wasn't.

Tying a quick knot in the top, he dashed back into the bedroom and removed the other lace from his running shoe. He tied the baggie around the lace, knotting it once and then a second time for good measure. Without wasting a single step, he grabbed the Voodoo doll, food, and makeshift salt necklace, and headed for Nichole's. He didn't even stop to smell the corpses this time, figuring if he ran into that one-eyed scary asshole, he'd just plow through. That skeleton looked fragile enough it would probably just fall apart.

And as disgusting as that thought was, it didn't matter. He needed to get to Nichole hours ago. The prospect of wearing a little rotting flesh wasn't going to deter him.

Fully expecting to find Nichole fast asleep, Julien opened the door carefully. He didn't want her to experience another second of whatever tortured her. He wanted to have everything prepped and ready when she woke.

The cabin was an icebox. It couldn't be more than fifty degrees inside. Shivering, he went to the thermostat, turning it back to a respectable sixty-five. He set the food and supplies on the table. Not only was the place colder than Santa's balls, it was spotless. Meth-addict-on-a-bender spotless.

Something was wrong. Not that the cabin had been messy before, but it didn't sparkle like this. And she should still be out. He might be used to the Valium/booze combo, but she wasn't.

Heart in his shoes, he dashed unto the bedroom where he'd left Nichole. Not only was she no longer in bed, but the comforter was pulled so tightly across the mattress, quarters would probably bounce off it. Gunnery Sergeant Hartman would be proud.

Faint knocking sounded from the opposite side of the room, like a branch hitting the side of the house in a windstorm, only more regular, like a heartbeat.

He could feel his face twist into a grimace as he padded around the bed, hating what was probably waiting for him.

It was exactly as he suspected, yet somehow much, much worse. Knees drawn to her chest, tears squeezing from beneath eyes clamped tightly shut, Nichole rocked back and forth, banging her head rhythmically against the wall.

He knelt beside her, placing a hand gently on her knee. Oblivious, she continued to rock, her breathing forced and labored.

It was until he gave her knee a firm shake that she finally opened her eyes.

As if the lids were a cap trapping the tears, they burst forth with a vengeance as she flung herself into his arms.

"They won't stop! Julien, I can't make them stop!"

His arms wrapped tightly around her shoulders as she buried her head in his chest. "I know," he whispered, gently stroking her back. "I'm here to help."

"I don't know what you can do! They just won't stop talking! The noise, the constant noise..." Her hands flew to her ears and she began rocking again.

He hugged her tighter. Her tears broke his heart, but with every sniffle, he became more and more determined to help her.

Placing his hands on her shoulders, he reluctantly peeled her back and stooped to look directly into her eyes. "I *can* help," he insisted. "Do you trust me?"

She offered him a confused nod.

"Good. Let's get you back into that salt circle."

Easing her to her feet, he helped her to the center of the salt circle and gently guided her down. After making sure the scattered line of salt was perfectly intact, he knelt beside her and pulled scissors stolen from the first aid kit from his pocket. She looked frightened and wary, but he couldn't worry about that now. He had a job to do.

Voodoo rituals weren't his strength, but he knew just about everything about them. Mostly from years of watching Grandmere, and to a lesser extent, his mother, and some from the copious amount of research he'd done over the years. It was all in theory though. He'd never actually performed a single ritual.

"I need a lock of your hair—"

Concern in her troubled eyes, a hand flew to her midnight locks.

"It doesn't have to be very thick," he reassured her. "No more than a pencil width, maybe an inch or two. I'll take it from the back and underneath."

"Why—"

He smiled. "The Voodoo doll."

That didn't ease the tension from her eyes, but she nodded anyway. She tilted her head forward and lifted the bulk of hair from her neck. Taking a narrow clump of the silky strands between his fingers, he snipped a couple inches off the bottom and then rose. He'd love to spend more time with his hands in her hair, but that would have to wait for another time.

In spite of their current situation, he was hopeful it would happen sometime in the near future.

"Don't go anywhere," he told her. "I'll be right back."

Running to the kitchen, he grabbed the supplies from the table and then rushed back to the bedroom. Nichole was just as he'd left her: kneeling on the floor, looking completely confused and bewildered. The pained expression on her face and deep furrows between her manicured brows told him her torment was no less severe than it had been hours ago.

Hoping to offer reassurance, he knelt beside her. "I know this all seems overwhelming," he said as he pulled out the Voodoo doll and pins. "But hopefully it'll all be better soon."

Using the white-tipped pin he'd found in the emergency sewing kit, he secured the lock of her hair to the top of his makeshift Voodoo doll. In reality, Voodoo dolls in nature *were* makeshift. He was so used to commercially made dolls, it was weird thinking of using one so haphazardly tossed together.

It would do. It would have to. He had three points of protection: the salt circle, the Voodoo doll, and the white candle. It *had* to work.

After relighting the candle, he placed a hand on her shoulder reassuringly. "Are you ready?"

Still looking just as baffled as ever, her head moved up and down in agreement.

As hesitant as it was, he'd take it. He held the loose end of her hair attached to the doll's cork head and Sharpie face over the flame until it caught fire, and then lifted it up, side to side and around Nichole's kneeling frame.

"By all the high ones, worlds and wise," he chanted, "by oceans afar and of the deep blue skies, by day and night and powers three, silence is my will, thus grant it be."

Almost immediately, Nichole's face contorted and her hands flew to her ears. "Julien...?"

At the same time, faint howling sounded in the distance. At first, he thought he might be imagining it, but within seconds he realized it wasn't his imagination, but wind.

It whipped through the room. Less a breeze than a stream of concentrated air. The candle flickered as it swirled around the room, curtains and bedspread fluttering as it passed.

"Julien...?" Nichole's voice was pleading, and whatever was going on her head was obviously not pleasant. But the ritual must be doing something. He couldn't stop now.

"By all the high ones, worlds and wise," he repeated, "by oceans afar and of the deep blue skies, by day and night and powers three, silence is my will, thus grant it be!"

"Julien...?"

God, her voice. She sounded so desperate, so afraid.

But the wind picked up, the howling increasing in pitch until it was a whistle so shrill it was almost painful. It was definitely painful for Nichole. Her face contorted in pure agony and her hands pressed so tightly against her ears the flesh burned red beneath them.

But it had to be working. Had to be.

One more time, he'd give it one more time. Three was supposed to be the charm…

Dipping the Voodoo doll hair in the wildly dancing candle flame so it continued to burn, Julien repeated the gesture with the doll and the chant. As he spoke, the wind increased in velocity until he had to shout to be heard over it.

"Julien!" Nichole screamed, tears streaming down her face.

With his free hand, he grabbed the salt necklace and placed it over her head just as the screeching wind whipped past, extinguishing the candle flame and the doll's hair at the same time.

And then everything fell silent.

Except for the ringing in his ears.

The smell of burnt hair lingered in the air, mingling with the sulfur smoke billowing from the candle wick. Curtains settled back into place in the suddenly still air and Nichole's hands slowly lowered as her tears shifted to those of gratitude instead of pain and horror.

"Oh!" she breathed. "Julien..." A smile spread over her face. "You did it!"

She fell into him and after tossing the Voodoo doll aside, he gladly wrapped his arms around her. She settled quite nicely into his embrace and he rested his cheek on the top of her head. Lavender and vanilla wafted up from her hair. Usually so neatly contained; it now flowed wildly over her shoulders and down her back.

"I can't believe you did it," she murmured. "They're quiet. They're finally quiet."

He'd like to say he'd come up with the combination of spells on his own, but the one was a standard Voodoo protection spell, he just modified it a tad. And Grandmere had put a salt necklace together once for his mother. He remembered the day quite clearly even though he'd only been eight at the time. The parallels to this evening were startling—his mother, rocking in the corner and screaming at the silent room to shut up until Grandmere stepped in. Delia Villere still wore that salt necklace to this day.

"Sorry for the makeshift dime bag as an accessory," he said. "It's all I could find."

She peeled back and glanced down at her "necklace," most likely seeing it for the first time. She was grinning when she glanced back up. "It's beautiful."

"It seems to be working at least."

Gaze lingering on his, her grin slowly dropped until it was sly and half-cocked. He knew that look. He'd been waiting not so patiently to see it on her face again. Like he had at the gazebo. Like he had earlier.

Rising to her knees, she slid one hand around his neck and brought the other to his chest. Leaning forward, she pressed her lips against his in a soft, delicate embrace.

That didn't last.

The hand at his chest twisted in his shirt, and she pulled him closer as her tongue eased into his mouth. He could feel the passion rising with every pass of her soft, wet lips. It stirred an equal passion in him, one he was having a hard time containing.

Tossing a leg over his lap, she pushed against him with enough force he had to drop and arm to brace his body. Her hips undulated against him and he knew his cock was rock hard. There sure as fuck wasn't a way to prevent it.

But she merely whimpered and undulated again, her kiss deepening even further.

And then she peeled off her shirt, returning immediately to devouring him with passion.

"Jesus," he muttered.

Kiss never letting up, hips still rocking against him, she reached behind her back and unhooked her bra.

He couldn't believe what he was about to do, but he had to say something. He wanted her…bad, but he needed to make sure it was the right time.

"Nichole…"

One shoulder shrugged out of the bra.

"…are you…"

Then the other.

"…sure…"

The bra was tossed aside.

"Yes," she said into his lips. "Absolutely, yes."

That was about all the argument he had in him.

He trailed his hand down her smooth back until it cupped her perfectly round ass. With a squeeze, he pulled her against his cock, now straining against the confines of his pants.

"Mmm," she breathed, pausing to grind against him one last time before rising to her feet.

Her breasts were as perfect as her ass. Round, full, and perched perkily over a narrow waist. She stepped out of the salt circle, walking backward until her legs hit the edge of the bed. With her index finger, she gestured for him to follow.

He did, yanking off his shirt as he went.

Placing her palms on his chest, she ran both hands down and up again. "Very nice," she said.

Before he could make a smartass comment, she spun and pushed him backward onto the mattress. A sly grin on her lips, she took a few steps back and then, looping her thumbs in the belt loops of her shorts, coyly bent over, sliding them and her panties off in one smooth swoop.

His swallow was so thick, he had to force it down. He cleared his throat. "Damn, girl, you are gorgeous."

Kicking out of the garments, she slinked back toward him, dropping to her knees at his feet. Unhooking the button of his pants, she said, "I could say the same thing about you."

"Good to know we're on the same page."

"Uh huh."

His pants unzipped and her fingers hooked in the waistband, she gave a little tug and he lifted his ass briefly off the mattress so she could pull off the slacks. She did, removing his shoes at the same time.

Once he was as naked as she was, she snuck her shoulders between his knees, placed her hands on either side of his ass, and gave him a sly look before running her tongue lightly up the length of his shaft.

Both hands fell behind him this time. He needed all the help he could not to lose it.

When she reached the tip, she glanced up at him with those damn seductress eyes and said, "I know you have a condom."

"I brought it just for you."

"Uh huh."

"I carry one in my wallet. For emergencies."

"Of course." Her tongue ran back down his shaft before she pulled back, dipping into his pants pocket and pulling out the wallet and then the condom. She tossed the wallet aside.

With her teeth, she tore the wrapper off and it joined the wallet on the floor. Wrapping a soft hand around his cock, she slid the condom smoothly down his length.

"You're good at that," he noted.

That sly grin just wouldn't leave her face. "I like control," she said as she climbed onto the bed and straddled his lap.

That much was apparent. And understandable. Knowing what she was, what she could do, what she was constantly surrounded by… Of course she liked control. It explained so much about her personality.

He leaned back on his arms and took her in. She was like this little sex goddess. If he hadn't already tasted that pent-up passion in the gazebo, he would have been shocked. Pent-up was the key word and he knew it. She probably spent so much time trying to keep the demons at bay that every desire in her body crawled just under her skin, begging to be released. Clearly, he was her release.

He was happy to receive it.

"Control away," he drawled.

Hands cupping his shoulders, she made this amazingly sexy purring noise as she slid onto his cock. Hips rolling up and down, breasts brushing his chest with each rise and fall of her body, she rested her cheek against his, her mouth right by his ear so that every breath, every whimper, every moan of pleasure was amplified.

"Mmm, Julien, you feel so good." Her husky whisper was like an extra hand stroking his cock.

"If you keep talking like that I'm going to come."

"Good," she murmured. "Me too." Her hips pushed harder against him, her sex grinding deliciously against his skin.

Fuck. Fuck, fuck, fuck, fuck, fuck.

He refused to come before her, holding back his orgasm until it was painful. Even though he'd happily finish her off with his tongue, finger, whatever she wanted, he knew she needed to control her own release. Knew this was part of her therapy from the hell plaguing her the better part of the night. He wouldn't deny her an ounce of control.

Thankfully, it wasn't long before her nails dug into his flesh, her moans increased, and the clenching of her core sent him into overdrive, his own orgasm slamming into hers.

She pulled back slightly to kiss him, hands gently cupping his face, her hips stilling as the last pumps of his orgasm trailed off. He eased forward, taking the weight off his arms so he could wrap them around her back. He wasn't sure what was going to happen next, but whatever she needed, he was more than ready to provide.

CHAPTER FIFTEEN

Pushing damp hair out of her face, she nuzzled contentedly into the hollow where his neck met his shoulder. There was something about the smell of his skin that was calming. Which was good because as the hormone-fueled sexual adrenaline wore off, she began to doubt herself.

Not that she was normally shy in the bedroom, but she didn't usually attack her lovers so aggressively. But between the stress of the endless voices and the immense relief granted by this gorgeous, sexy man, something simply clicked in her brain. Knowing Julien would be an eager participant certainly helped fuel that release. She didn't regret anything. It felt too good to let go.

"Thank you for stopping the voices," she whispered into his flesh after a few moments. Perhaps it didn't have to be said, but she wanted to anyway. "I don't know what would have happened if you hadn't come when you did." She was astounded he'd been able to help at all, but she didn't begin to know how to voice that appreciation.

"I thought the sex was a pretty solid thank you," he said, pressing his lips to her hair. "But you're welcome."

Leave it to Julien to make light of the situation. If she was honest with herself, she'd acknowledge it was exactly what she needed. In spite of the horrors of the last few hours, she was far too serious far too often. Julien's humor helped anchor her.

Still, she peeled back and gave him a "look". He, of course, wore a half-cocked grin. "You're an ass," she said.

"I know." He kissed her chin playfully. "And you like it."

"Hmph."

"Come here." Pulling her back in, he eased back onto the mattress, taking her with him as he lay against the pillows.

She was happy to settle into the crook of his arm. Closing her eyes, she snuggled her body a little closer to him, smiling to herself when his arm pulled her even tighter. The steady beat of his heart, slow and strong beneath his chest, was a soothing lullaby in her ears. It felt so good to be held. The relief was overwhelming. Enough to bring every raw emotion boiling to the surface. If she wasn't careful, she was going to bawl like a baby.

What did he know about her abilities? How did he know? Obviously, he knew *something*, otherwise he wouldn't have known what to do. There were so many unanswered questions and she didn't know where to begin. Or even how to begin. How did she explain she could see ghosts and communicate with them? Broaching that subject was scary, unchartered territory.

She touched the bag of salt at her neck for reassurance.

"I think we should talk about..." Pausing, she tried to mentally recite the words before they exited her mouth. She failed. "I mean, I guess I should explain why I was a total wreck this morning."

"You're a medium," he said nonchalantly. "You communicate with spirits in some form or another. Clairaudient, judging from what I saw."

She was pretty sure she stopped breathing. It was hard enough admitting the abilities to herself, but to hear them so casually announced...

Craning her neck, she stared at him.

"My mother," he said by way of explanation, still as nonplussed as ever. "She even runs séances out of our home in New Orleans for those wanting to communicate with their loved ones. For a fee, of course. Most of it's fake, but she does have abilities."

"Oh." Her mind raced. His mother...his *mother* also communicated with ghosts? Between that and the Voodoo and the ritual? It was just so overwhelming. How much should she tell him?

She'd always fought to keep her sensitivities a secret, even managing to keep them hidden from past boyfriends and friends. She worked hard to make sure people thought she was a normal, everyday woman. It felt weird that divulging that secret to him had been so effortless, so natural. She hated all the crazy and insane details of what she could do. Wouldn't he?

"So, what went wrong?" he said, bringing her back to him. "You lost control, right? You couldn't shut them out like you usually do?"

Slowly she nodded, studying his face. His expression wasn't the least bit alarmed, startled, shocked, or judgmental. This was everyday life to him. No big deal.

If there was ever someone she could tell, it appeared Julien Villere was her man.

"Yeah," she muttered, easing her head back on his shoulder. If she was going to spill her guts to him, she didn't want to risk catching the expression on his face. Just in case. "I don't know what went wrong. It's different here...not like in Baton Rouge, where suppressing the voices and sightings comes naturally."

"So you're clairvoyant too?"

She nodded into his shoulder. "I've had 'the gift' since..." She grimaced. How she hated that word. "...since around the time I was in kindergarten. But by the time I was eleven, I'd learned how to make them—the ghosts—stay away. For the most part anyway. I can always feel them. That's how I know Daddy isn't dead. If he were dead I'd be able to sense it." She sighed. "I've kept the ability locked away for so long, I haven't actually *seen* or talked to a ghost in years."

"Until last night."

"Right. I wanted to contact them because they see everything. I thought they might help." She shook her head. "They completely overwhelmed me. And then I couldn't make it stop. Somehow, I was able to shut them out visually, but they were still in my head." Pain pierced her temples as she remembered. Shuddering, she lifted her head to look at him. "Without you, I don't know what would have happened."

"I'm just glad I *was* able to help."

She studied his face. So calm, so relaxed. "I can't believe this doesn't freak you out," she said.

His free shoulder shrugged. "My family has a colorful past and some interesting...skills."

"Well, it freaks me out."

"I can see that." He let out an amused chortle. "That might be a lot of your problem. From what I understand about ghosts, they prey on weakness."

"I know. I thought the protective items would be enough."

"Not if the ghosts are very strong."

"How do you know so much?"

Darkness washed over his face before being replaced with a bitter smile. "I recently had my own run-in with a long dead relative. Under her control, I did some pretty awful things. If I hadn't been so bitter and angry, I don't think she could have gotten into my head the way she did."

She wanted to ask more, wanted to understand what horrors he could possibly be referring to. Suddenly desiring nothing more than to understand every detail, good or bad, about him, she opened her mouth to ask the questions when he interrupted her with, "What's in the swamp?"

She wasn't prepared for that question, and her jaw hung agape for a few moments before she forced it closed and swallowed. "You saw *it*, didn't you?" The words came out in a meek whisper.

"I just about ran into it. Reeked like nothing else. Half skeleton, half rotting flesh."

Ice cold chills prickled her skin and she pushed closer to Julien's strong, warm body.

"Why are there walking corpses in the swamp, Nichole? It wasn't just the one I saw tonight, the one that's obviously been around the block a few times. We saw one the first day we went out in the swamp, didn't we? On the way back from your daddy's fishing hole? And when we were at the dock, I saw something in the distance and it completely freaked you out. Was that one too?"

She both nodded and shook her head at the same time. "Probably the one you saw tonight. It's more…active. But they aren't dead," she told him. "The White Eyes. They're something…but they aren't dead. I mean, I'd sense the ghost if they were. And I don't sense anything." Just thinking about them made her body tense.

His eyes narrowed as he absorbed her words. "Shay said they were zombies."

"I don't know."

"Is that why you're so scared of the swamp?"

She nodded, lowering her head back to his shoulder. The heat rolling off his body was comforting as she lay next to him, making her feel safe for the first time since her father disappeared. Safe enough to tell him a story she hadn't repeated in over thirteen years. Even so, knowing what she was about to say filled her with dread.

"I saw the first one when I was twelve," she started slowly, quietly. "I took Daddy's boat out to crawdad. The sun was just starting to rise and I was heading for the final trap when I saw him standing off in the distance. It was this old man, Claude Gautreaux, who'd been missing for over a week. I overheard my daddy and Wendell discussing it a few days before. He was a known drunk and everyone assumed he was dead." She paused to take a deep breath. "But there he was, just standing there in the swamp. I called his name and he didn't respond. I thought maybe he was hurt. So I took the boat, and when I got a little closer I could tell—"

She cut herself off with a bite of her lip. It was hard to repeat, even after so many years, even feeling like she could trust Julien with her secret.

"He was alive, sort of. I guess. I mean, he was breathing. But it was like he was catatonic. He just seemed…empty. And his eyes…milky white, never focusing or even blinking…only staring. And then I saw the other one."

Just talking about that horrifying image began making her shiver a little.

Julien squeezed her closer, the tips of his fingers gently stroking her arm. His touch, his warmth, felt so good. It felt good to have him close, to have someone actually listen, to have someone she could talk to.

"It was just like you described. A walking corpse. Rotting flesh literally falling from the bone. But not dead. Not a ghost. But just as empty as Claude." She shuddered again, her throat so dry she could barely swallow. Determined to keep going, she rolled over, reaching for the glass of water on the nightstand. She took a sip, and then another, before turning back to him.

Propped on the pillow with one arm tucked behind his head, still completely naked just as she was, he watched her intently.

"Are you sure you aren't freaked out?"

"By the undead living rotting empty things in the swamp? A little."

"By me."

"No, of course not."

The look of genuine concern on his face made her almost forget where she left off. If she wasn't careful, he was going to make her want him in a permanent way.

Clearing her throat, she took another drink of water before returning the glass to the nightstand and easing back onto the bed beside him. She stayed turned on her side, leaning on her elbow with her head cradled in her hand. She searched his face for a moment, looking for any sign of doubt. There was none, only understanding. The connection she felt to him was truly remarkable. To be able to share this...

"I immediately went to tell Gran. She is...was...my daddy's mama and the only person who truly understood my...abilities. She had them too. She used to live across the main road in this dinky white house that backs up to the levee. Daddy rents it out now. Or did." She paused. God, did she actually just use past tense talking about him? Her face twisted into a frown. "Anyway," she went on, "she didn't say much at the time other than I should keep it to myself. For some reason I felt like she knew more than what she was telling me. Looking back, it was probably for my own protection. I didn't say anything for a few days. But then I kept thinking about poor Claude, trapped in the swamp with that...thing. And would he have the same fate? Rotting and unresponsive but still somehow alive? I kept trying to figure out what I saw. It was—is—still so hard to grasp.

"I don't know why, but one day at school when kids were joking about how old drunk Claude must've rolled out of the ditch he was sleeping in and into an alligator's mouth, I just blurted it. Told them the whole ridiculous story. Of course no one believed me. And the more they doubted, the more I tried to convince them. From that day forward, I was the butt of a lot of jokes, and pretty much the entire town started calling me "Ghost Girl" or whispering and snickering whenever I walked into a room. At the time, it was pretty traumatizing. I mean, I was twelve. The nickname followed me to high school. I'm shocked it didn't follow me to Baton Rouge. To this day, I don't talk about it—to anyone."

With the end of the revelation, a wall of fatigue suddenly hit her. Like the weight of the memory had been a physical burden for the last half of her life and now that she'd dropped it, she could finally rest.

He rolled on his side, his posture mimicking hers. With his free hand, he picked up the lock of hair dangling in her eyes, his fingers smoothing the strands as he gently lifted it away from her face and placed it over her shoulder. "Well, I'm honored you trust me enough to share it with me."

If she didn't feel like she was going to collapse any moment, she would have pounced on him again. His sex appeal was growing by the second. Unfortunately, her arm could no longer support the boulder that was her head.

She melted onto the pillow, barely able to cover her mouth as she yawned. "I'm sorry," she murmured. "I'm just…so…tired all of the sudden."

"No worries," he said as he eased to the bed, sharing her pillow. "I know you must be exhausted."

Her eyes were already started to close. Like a good two-year-old, she tried to fight it. "You're going to stay, right?"

"Of course."

She hoped the muscles in her face were strong enough to lift the corners of her mouth so he could see her smile. At least she was able to force out the word, "Good," before her eyelids won the battle and darkness overtook her.

CHAPTER SIXTEEN

René stared at his father in absolute shock. Standing casually in the foyer, he brushed rain droplets from his overcoat, with two, wide-eyed little girls huddled behind him.

At first René was deceived by their fair skin and light-brown ringlets. But the moment one looked at him with her deep, dark brown eyes, he knew.

These were his father's bastard children. The ones he'd conceived with that...mistress he kept in New Orleans.

René had never met the girls, but he was well aware of him. He couldn't fault Father for wanting comfort after Mother died, but he'd never understood the appeal of that Voodoo woman.

"What is this," he asked, stepping into the foyer while trying to avoid looking at the children now clutched to his father's side.

"I could not leave them. Their mother..." Pascal Grisé shook his head. "She isn't well, René. Ever since her brother's death..." He shook his head again. The worry lines were deep around his eyes, the fatigue apparent by the way his shoulders slumped.

"But it's been two years since he died."

"And she is worse now. Consumed by hatred. She isn't the same woman." He handed his coat to the servant waiting expectantly. *"I feared for the girls' safety."*

"With their own mother?" In spite of his aversion, he found himself staring at the girls. They oldest couldn't be more than six, the youngest maybe four.

"Yes. I heard rumors—and I believe them after seeing her firsthand—that she killed the American man thought to have shot her brother. The rumors are just that, and the police cannot find fault, but her anger is palpable. I don't doubt it." Pascal gestured for the servant. *"Warm some milk and biscuits,"* he told her. *"And find some warm clothes for my children. Make up the guest room adjacent to mine."*

"Yessir." The servant nodded before scampering away.

René could not believe his ears. *"You cannot mean for them to stay?"*

Wrapping his arm around her small shoulder, Father hugged the child closest to him. *"Of course I do."* He gave her ringlets a gentle stroke before turning to René, his only son. *"These are my daughters. Your sisters. I will not abandon them."*

He started for the great room. The eldest child stayed at his heels, but the youngest held back. *"Come, Sophie. There's a fire. You may dry off and have a bite to eat."* She hesitated a moment before jogging to catch up.

She grasped his leg. *"Where is mama?"* she asked.

Sadness washed over Father's features, the weariness deepening. "She is sick, child. Do not worry over it. Your sister isn't worried. Are you, Constance?"

The eldest shook her head, but the tears were obvious in her brown eyes. She took Sophie's hand.

"You say she murdered an American," René said as Father coaxed the young ones toward the other room. "That she isn't well after her brother's death. What makes you think this," he gestured toward the girls, "won't anger her? You don't think she'll come here looking for them?"

"Do not fret, René. She will not come here. It is too far and difficult a journey for a woman to make alone."

In spite of his father's reassurance, René could not imagine a woman driven to murder over the death of her brother wouldn't move heaven and earth to retrieve her children.

But he had to trust his father's judgment, even if he had his doubts.

Her eyes flashed open when a cool breeze lifted the hair from her neck. Remaining perfectly still, she panned the room, her gaze reluctant to focus as she searched for movement. The cream colored sheers were motionless against the closed blinds and she glanced toward the window unit. It was too far away to feel any circulation and even the ceiling fan was turned off. Other than the light rain hitting the tin roof, the room was silent.

Her eyes rested on Julien lying next to her, his slow, steady breathing indicating he was sound asleep.

With a muted grunt, she sat up. The room felt unnaturally still, the air almost stagnant, which made the breeze that woke her seem more like a dream.

Rubbing her eyes, she glanced at the glowing green numbers on the bedside clock. "Four-eleven." Considering she'd only been asleep for a few hours, it was too early to wake naturally. She took inventory of her body. Did she have to pee? No. Was she hungry? Not really. Maybe she was thirsty...

Her body still clumsily slow, she reached over and fumbled for the water glass on the nightstand, nearly dropping it as she lifted it to her mouth. Why did the air in the room feel so thick and heavy? It was just too quiet.

That was it. Not only were the irritatingly loud voices of a hundred ghosts gone from her head, she couldn't feel the ghosts at all. Not even a trace. It made her feel cut off, somehow, like trying to run as fast as possible through a pool of water. And she felt almost...empty.

She should be happy for the reprieve—and she was—but the lack of their presence, which was always so constant at the plantation, made her feel like a stranger in her own skin. It was like she was suddenly very much alone.

Except she wasn't. Julien slept peacefully beside her. Returning the water to its spot beside the clock, she scooted down and snuggled close to him. His warmth was like a soothing embrace and she relaxed into it.

She'd been running from her abilities for most of her life, but now was a time she needed them, especially if she was going to find Daddy. Julien would figure out what to do. He'd been able to shut out of the voices; she was confident he could help her retrieve, and then control them.

Closing her eyes, she tried to ease her mind back into sleep. It wasn't easy. Heaviness pulled at her lids, but her mind raced. Normally, the constant presence of ghosts was like white noise. With their absence, the stillness was nearly deafening.

Julien's body next to hers might be soothing, but that he felt so amazing was almost more distracting. It was a little frightening. She usually fought so hard to keep her guard up—both emotional and with her abilities—especially with men. The idea of getting close to someone just to have them run away when they discovered she could talk to the dead was terrifying.

Julien might be different, but the prospect of letting him into her life still scared her. She was hopeful, but she was also undeniably cautious.

"I can help you find your daddy," a woman's voice, thick with a French accent, cooed in her ear. It sounded like the spirit from the day before, the one that seemed to want to help. But this wasn't a thought, or the internal murmuring of ghosts, or a simple *feeling*. It was an actual voice that smashed through the silence like shattering glass.

Startled, she bolted up. "Who's there?" she whispered.

The fuzzy outline of a woman stood in the doorway, backlit by dim moonlight. Her arms extended forward. "Come. I 'ave seen him."

With her abilities silenced, Nichole couldn't tell who, or what, the woman was. She palmed her eyes and rubbed in an attempt to refocus and ascertain whether she might be dreaming. When she looked up, the woman was still there, her beautiful eyes rimmed with concern as she reached out both hands.

The gesture pulled instinctively at her. She *must* be a ghost who'd broken through Julien's protection spells, answering Nichole's plea for help.

And she had to respond. Daddy deserved that and much more.

Pushing back the bed covers, she rose. The wood floor creaked as she took her first step, jolting her into reality. Was she just going to follow this…apparition?

Twisting her body, she turned back to the bed. Julien hadn't moved. Dim light from the alarm clock bathed the silhouette of his handsome face in a soft green glow.

She struggled with her emotions to leave him. He'd given her so much and protected her from so much. Maybe she should wake him…

"Your father is waiting."

She shifted back to the woman at the door. When their eyes locked, Nichole found herself completely mesmerized. Whether it was the woman's beauty, or the intensity of her deep brown gaze, she found she couldn't look away. The pull to come closer intensified until Nichole found it impossible to keep her feet from moving. With each step, a whirling breeze pushed her forward until she took the woman's icy hand.

Walking felt like floating as the woman guided her down the porch steps, and she had to keep reminding herself she was awake. It certainly felt real, but how could she be sure? Her whole life was based on things most people couldn't see or even understand. Things she barely understood.

A gentle tug pulled at her mind, wiping out her thoughts. The path leading to the swamp, still warm from the heat of the day, felt wonderful on her cool feet. Like looking through a fish-eye camera lens, she glanced down at them, noting with little interest that she wasn't wearing shoes.

Shouldn't she be wearing shoes? Somewhere in the depths of her mind, a voice warned that walking barefoot toward the swamp was a bad idea, but it was shoved beneath the intoxicating need to follow the woman and find Daddy. Things like shoes were trivial.

The tiny voice in the back of her mind fought back. It screamed for her to run back to the cabin, back to the safety of Julien's warm body still lying in her bed. But somehow the desire to keep going overrode the warning, no matter how shrill and desperate it became.

Frogs calling to potential mates joined the voice in her head, growing louder and louder as her steps slowed. At the same time, the urge to run grew stronger and stronger. She had barely acknowledged the desire to flee when the woman abruptly stopped and so did she. Wetness splashed up her legs and hands and she blinked in shock.

Shaking her head to clear it, she tried to make sense of what was happening. She stood calf-deep in the bayou, mud squished between her toes. In the moonlit water's reflection, she caught a glimpse of her naked body. Somewhere in the distance, drumming joined the chorus of frogs.

The urge to run took over. She started to turn when someone grabbed her from behind, pinning her arms behind her back. Struggling against their iron-strong grasp, she tried to twist away, turning just enough to catch a glimpse of her assailant.

Pain shot through her gut, knocking the breath from her lungs. Everything started spinning out of control. "Daddy?"

Expression flat, he didn't acknowledge or even look at her. He just stared straight ahead while keeping her arms tightly locked in his.

"Daddy, what are you doing? Let me go!"

Again, he didn't respond, no matter how hard she struggled. Why wouldn't he answer her?

And then she saw it. His eyes were pure white, glowing dully against his dark skin.

What was left of her guts twisted in agony.

From the corner of her eye, she caught a glimpse of the beautiful woman, lips curled in a half-smile, before she disintegrated into the night. Behind her, a wake of pure evil filled the air like smoke.

Oh God. What had she done?

The stench hit her before she saw the massive outline of his body. She never did quite see his face, but she knew immediately who approached.

"Two-Tooth," she mouthed, the words trapped with her breath.

He jerked her out of Daddy's grasp and into his. World still spinning, she tried pulling away when warm, rancid breath whispered in her ear, "Looks like I got me a present."

A chemical odor wrapped around her nose like a vice, overpowering her before she could make a sound. Black dots dominated her vision until darkness took over.

CHAPTER SEVENTEEN

Julien turned over and reached for Nichole, his hand feeling nothing but empty space and cool sheets. With heavy lids, his eyes opened halfway, gaze clumsily shifting left then right.

"Nichole?" he whispered.

Silence.

Pushing back the blankets, he rose, rubbing his sore arm absently as he stepped over clothes still scattered on the floor, and walked toward the bathroom, half expecting to catch her on the toilet.

"Hey, it's me. You decent?" he asked, staying just behind the door to give her privacy.

Still no answer.

With a turn of the knob, he peeked his head around the corner and pushed open the door. Lights off, there was no evidence that she had used it recently.

Returning to the bedroom, he scooped up his clothing and began to dress. Like lonely, discarded toys, Nichole's clothes remained on the floor where they'd been left the night before. Nagging doubt began to churn in his gut and a quick walk through the cabin confirmed she was definitely gone. Her purse remained. And the gun still sat unsafely on the kitchen counter.

Julien wasn't normally a worrier, but something felt *off*. She'd been such a mess when he'd found her sobbing last night, and while the protection spell seemed to work, what if it had somehow worn off? What if it was only a temporary fix? He might be familiar with protection spells but he certainly wasn't rehearsed.

On the other hand, she might have simply gone up to the main house for breakfast, because judging by the loud grumbling coming from his own stomach, the woman probably—definitely—needed to eat.

Nerves calmed by the thought, he slipped on his shoes and headed straight for the main house. Like a little boy searching for a lost puppy, he scanned the grounds for any sign of her. When gut wrenching urgency flooded his thoughts and made him want to sprint the rest of the way to the house, he actually had to take a few deep breaths to keep his cool. With any luck, he'd find her enjoying a plateful of scrambled eggs with bacon.

He climbed the side stairs to the wraparound porch three at a time, willing himself to slow down as he stepped into the house. The front parlor was alive with chatter from people sitting in overstuffed wingbacks, discussing the goings on of the daily paper and sipping their complimentary coffee. He nodded to a few of the guests, attempting to look inconspicuous while peering into rooms. They all came up empty, including the dining room.

Which only made his stomach feel like a washing machine filled with rocks when it grumbled in response to the aroma of breakfast wafting through the air.

The door to the kitchen was halfway open, and he could hear Miss Puts' annoying voice dominating over the sound of clanging dishes. He carefully glanced through the door, hoping he wouldn't be spotted. The old bag wasn't someone he wanted to deal with.

Unfortunately, not only was the kitchen missing Nichole, but Puts spotted him immediately.

"What can I help you with, darlin'?" She shuffled over, a pleasant looking fake smile on her overpowered face. "You know you ain't s'posed to be in here."

As much as he didn't want to deal with her, it probably wouldn't hurt to ask. "Have you seen Nichole this morning?"

Artificial red curls didn't move a millimeter as she shook her head. "You check the cabin?"

"Of course." He tried not to let the irritation seep into his tone.

"You notice if her car is gone?"

One, the cars were kept in a separate lot away from the manor. And two, he'd never even seen her car.

"No, but her purse is still in the cabin."

Her smile turned genuine, then sly, like she'd just received a bit of juicy gossip and was giddy about it. She shrugged hefty shoulders. "I don't know if that'd stop her. That girl is prone to flake out at the strangest times. Always been like that. I wouldn't be surprised if she's halfway back to Baton Rouge by now. Purse or no purse."

His teeth hurt he clenched his jaw so tightly. What a miserable old—

"Though you might check with Wendell," she interrupted with a dismissive wave of her hand that was directed as much at him as it was Nichole's whereabouts. "She sometimes likes to help him in the mornings."

He didn't waste a second getting out of there, tripping over the edge of the rug as he jogged through the parlor and out the front door, no longer giving two shits if he was conspicuous or not.

Something was wrong. He could feel it the way his organs contracted into pins and needles. He should have thought to set an alarm or something, just to keep a closer eye on her. When his mother had these episodes, she was a wreck for weeks.

But that was just it, he hadn't been thinking clearly. All he could think about at the time was helping her. And then she'd seduced him. Of course he'd be distracted by his cock and selfish desires. He should've fucking taped that thing down.

Once his feet hit the pathway he broke into a full run, not slowing until he reached the utility shed. Thankfully Wendell was inside, loading cutting shears onto a trailer filled with miscellaneous landscaping equipment.

The old man stopped and looked at him. Eyebrows raised, his gaze scaled up and down. "What's the matter with you, boy? You look like the devil did your laundry."

Under normal circumstances, that might have made Julien laugh, but worry overrode his emotions. No matter how hard he tried, he couldn't seem to shake the acid churning in his belly.

"Have you seen Nic—" His voice broke slightly when he said her name. He cleared his throat. "Have you seen Nichole this morning?"

"Can't say that I have."

"Well if you see her, tell her I'm looking..." He paused. This was fucking ridiculous. He needed to stop pussyfooting and cut to the chase. "Wendell, Nichole is missing."

The geezer blinked, confused. "What'd ya mean she's missing?"

"I mean, she's nowhere to be found and trust me, I've scoured the entire plantation."

"Sorry, boy, you don't look much like her keeper. But no, I haven't seen her."

The acid had burned its way through his stomach and was now making quick work on his entrails.

Wendell started to turn away and Julien grabbed his arm, stopping him. "Look, old man—"

Bushy gray eyebrows raised, he glanced first at the hand on his arm and then at Julien.

With a breath to help unclench his jaw, Julien dropped his hand. "Sorry. I just...I just don't think you understand. I was, um..." He pursed his lips. Normally, he wasn't concerned with discretion, but it was different with Nichole. And as much as he hated discussing their *relationship*, as it was, he needed Wendell's help.

"I was with Nichole early this morning," he said, pausing to let the implication sink in. "And when I woke she was gone. All her stuff is still in the cabin and she doesn't seem to be anywhere. With her father missing…dead, whatever, and then yesterday we got chased out of the swamp via gunshot by those crazy backwoods Villeres…" He shook his head. "I just have this feeling—"

"Wait. You went out to the Villeres' place?"

"Yeah. Nichole took me. I'm here researching my family and—"

Wendell grunted. "Why you insist on snooping around…" He paused, walking to the shed doorway and peering out, glancing first toward the bayou and then around each side of the building. With another grunt, he turned his attention back to Julien. "Come with me, boy." His voice was low but firm.

Julien followed as Wendell led him to an office in the back of the shed, behind the tractor and through a door—which was promptly closed. Whatever Wendell was about to tell him, he obviously didn't want other ears to hear.

Unfortunately, it took him forever to start talking. Jaw sliding back and forth like a chewing cow, the grinding noise from his teeth audible, Wendell just stood there. Julien was about to crawl out of his skin. The longer he waited the longer Nichole was…

Well, actually, he had no idea. But this sure as hell wasn't helping him solve the mystery.

He was about to shake the words out of the man's mouth when Wendell finally spoke up. "You know anything about the Swamp Villeres?"

There was something about the way he said "Villere" made Julien's mouth go dry. It was almost accusatory.

"I didn't even know they existed until three days ago."

The old man nodded as if he believed him, but there was clearly a degree of distrust in his eyes. "Well, we don't talk much about this around here, but with Nichole gone missing and you insisting on snooping around..." He shook his head. "I think that should the first place you look."

"You think they might have her?"

"I don't know, boy, but it's mighty suspicious. Given they're into some weird Voodoo out there—"

"Wait. You mean they practice Voodoo?"

"I don't know *what* they're practicin', but it's some sorta black magic."

Julien raised his brows, his mind racing through the implication. He took a step backward toward the door, ready to find his way to the Villere shack.

Wendell leaned forward, the serious expression on his withered face forcing Julien's attention. "Don't be in such a rush, son. You need to be prepared when you head out there. Those folks...what they got goin' on ain't exactly legal."

"What are you talking about?" Unless they were performing some weird sacrifices, Julien couldn't imagine what Voodoo ritual would be illegal.

"Let's just say they're doin' a little chemistry without a laboratory."

Great. A bunch of meth-heads. Just what he needed.

"So you need to go back to Nichole's place and look in the bedroom closet, behind the clothes. Robert kept a gun case—"

"Yeah, yeah...I know." Impatient to get going, the words came out quickly, cutting Wendell off. He might not know where the gun case was hidden, but he knew where Nichole had left a handgun. But maybe he should check out that gun rack, too.

Mentally he started making a list of all the things he might need. He had no idea what to expect, but given everything that had transpired in the last couple of days, if he could fit the kitchen sink into his backpack he was sure as hell going to take it.

"Get ya a gun, and then take Robert's boat..." Pausing, he cocked his head. "I take you know where that is too?"

Julien nodded rapidly, anxious for him to continue.

Wendell turned to a map of the bayou displayed on the wall. "Head east about a mile and a half and cut the engine, then idle in the rest of the way. You gonna have to stay low, boy. They don't like strangers and they don't like people snooping."

He knew all too well how the Villeres welcomed unexpected guests. "If you know they're cooking meth out there, and you know they're dangerous, why the hell don't you call the police?"

Once again, Wendell appeared to be literally chewing on his own thoughts. "Because, boy," he said slowly, "they're family."

And suddenly all the pieces fell into place.

It all went back to Sanite Villere. Of fucking course.

It wasn't uncommon for a woman like Sanite to be the mistress of a white man. He'd never actually seen it in his research, but it was common at the time.

After all, both Sanite and Laurent were the bastard children of Benoît Villere. And then his nightmares. There was always a white man in them that came with a gambit of conflicted emotions. And then there was that gut-wrenching loss of children taken. He'd never understood it until now.

The Grisé sisters must be her children. That's why Grandmere had shrines built to them. And that made the swamp Villeres their descendants.

"So you did recognize the women in those pictures?" he said to Wendell. "They're the common connection, aren't they? Why the good ol' swamp Villeres are both my relatives and yours. Pascal Grisé had a little taboo affair with a mixed woman, my ancestor, Sanite Villere, and got a couple kids out of the deal. At one time they shared your family name. What happened? Let me guess, the Civil War?"

"It ain't somethin' I'm proud of. Yes, my great-great-great-granddaddy had an affair with Sanite. The story goes that he made her angry by takin' their girls after she went crazy, and when he wouldn't give 'em back, she cursed him and he disappeared into the swamp. Out of what I s'pose was sympathy, his son, René, took in his half-sisters, keeping 'em around as house servants. He died in the War, and when all the slaves were released, his own kids weren't so sympathetic and turned them away. Those girls had nowhere to go but out into the bayou. I think they took their mama's name at that point. The rest is history."

"Why didn't they return to New Orleans? My family, their family, was still there."

"I don't know. They had their own families here, and they were little when Pascal brought them here. This was probably all they knew. I do know they went out in the bayou."

"So, let me get this straight, now you protect a bunch of deviants out of guilt?"

"They might not be where they are if their ancestors weren't turned away from this plantation. We give 'em work. Try to keep them in line a little."

"And yet you hide the connection because you're ashamed."

"You know how it is down here. Folks don't often look kindly to mixin' things. 'Sides, I don't know what happened in the last couple hundred years, but they're just as crazy as their great-great-great grandmere. Probably the inbreeding."

Julien shook his head in disgust. Not just because of the blatant racism and the deceit, but also Wendell's misguided sense of obligation. One that now placed Nichole in danger.

He marched toward the door, yanking it open forcefully. "Well, you might want to come to terms with it all," he said, barely twisting his body toward the old man. "Because not only do I *not* feel any loyalty toward those fuckers, I intend to tell my family's *entire* story in my book. Even the not so pretty parts."

The metal door slammed behind him.

CHAPTER EIGHTEEN

Shrieking woke him. Inhuman noises that sounded more like the cries of a tortured animal than a person. René lay in bed for many minutes, trying to decipher what could make such an awful racket.

It took minutes of quiet breathing in the darkness to realize the shrieking actually consisted of words.

"You will give them back!" they cried. "You will give them back!"

Another noise joined the cries. A low voice, quiet and subdued compared to the chaos, although René knew the person must be shouting to be heard from his second story bedroom.

It took him a long moment to decipher pieces of the conversation. "They are not here... Please, calm yourself." And then even longer to realize the words came from Father.

And then everything went quiet. Gone was the inhuman screeching. Faintly he could hear chanting, the type often heard in the slave quarters. It did not comfort him. In fact, it made him fear for Father's safety.

Jumping up, René scrambled to the window, tripping over the bedpan and spilling the contents in the process. Peering through the glass, he had to squint to make out the figures on the lawn.

His back to the house, Father stood motionless before a woman. Her long, wild black hair loose, her hands held high, she gripped what looked like a doll in one hand and a small bottle in the other.

That had to be Sophie and Constance's mother. There could be no other explanation.

It may have been several years since his sisters had been retrieved from New Orleans, but René still remembered the fears he'd had over their abduction. Fears that were now coming true.

Shrugging into his robe, he rushed to the stairs. John stood at the doorway. A pistol clutched in his shaking hands, his wide eyes were a bright contrast against his dark skin. He seemed relieved when René approached, immediately handing him the gun.

"It is loaded, sir," he said.

René would have to reprimand him later for touching the family weapons, ones that should have been under lock and key, but at the moment he was thankful for the servant's impertinence.

He carefully checked over the pistol, verifying it was indeed loaded. He only prayed the servant had loaded it properly, should he actually need to use it.

Unfortunately, by the time he opened the door, it was too late. Father was gone. René strained his eyes peering into the darkness trying to locate him. But he seemed to have simply disappeared.

"What did you do to him?" he asked the woman.

Still chanting, the bottle clutched to her heart and the doll shredded to pieces at her feet, Sanite lifted her gaze to him. Her lips slowly spread into a malicious grin.

It wasn't the deviant way she smiled that made his heart pause, but the devil in her eyes.

Holding the gun outstretched, he walked onto the porch. "Tell me what you have done to him!"

"No," *she snarled.* "But you may share his fate."

He didn't feel his finger squeeze the trigger when she took a step forward. The shot managed to hit true and she flew backward, collapsing on the ground in a motionless heap. When blood saturated the front of her dress, he knew it was done, whether he'd meant it or not.

He turned to the house. John stood in the doorway, eyes wide as ever.

"Round up a crew to look for my father and then take the body down to the swamp and let the alligators deal with her."

John stared at the body and then back at René and then back at the body. He crossed himself several times, hands trembling like the wobbly legs of a newborn foal. "Sir, I—"

"Oh for heaven's sakes, I'll do it." *René shrugged out of his robe. Perhaps this was best anyway. At least he knew it would be done right and she and her witchcraft could become a permanent part of those murky waters. And no one would ever know what transpired here.*

Like waking up from a long, dreamless sleep, Nichole's consciousness slowly crept back into her brain and with it, her vision. She didn't actually open her eyes, she could just suddenly see. Sort of. Like looking through a fogged over window pane, the images were blurred and distorted.

Her eyes felt like they were filled with sand. As raw and painful as they were, she wondered when was the last time she blinked. She tried to, hoping to clear the blurred scene before her, but nothing happened.

She lifted her hand to rub them.

Still nothing.

Her heart leapt into action—the only thing that responded to her panic. Nothing else did. Not her legs when she begged them to move. Not her arms when she pleaded with them to do something, anything.

Any movement was impossible. It was like she was made of stone or encased up to her neck in quicksand. Merely a passenger in the vessel that was her body, no matter how loudly her mind screamed, the vessel refused to respond. Trapped. She was trapped.

As foggy as her vision was and as unresponsive her body was, her other senses were crystal clear. She could feel water lapping at her ankles, feel her heart beating in her chest, and hear every single creature down to the last cricket. Frogs and God knows what other kinds of creatures were nearly as loud as the ghosts had been in her head the night before. It was a buzz almost too loud to think through.

Or was that last night? How long had she been standing in the swamp? And where exactly was she?

Focusing all of her energy on peering through the haze obscuring her vision, she tried to absorb her surroundings. Weak light, the kind that followed the setting sun during dusk, bathed the trees around her in shadows. But it only confused her more. Had a full day already passed? Or was it morning? Was that the rising sun?

Not knowing was pure agony. Was she dead? Was she in the process of dying? Death would be so much better than this torture, this...nightmare.

Without warning or command from her body, her legs began to move. She could feel the muscles working, feel the way they heavily trudged through water and muck and mud, but there was absolutely nothing she could do to control them. Water splashed at her thighs and mosquitos feasted on her flesh, and all she could do was watch through a foggy window. The sound of drums in the distance increased in volume with each step she took, like a beacon drawing her in, one she was sure she should probably avoid but couldn't.

Many minutes later she lumbered into a homestead. She recognized it as belonging to the Swamp Villeres. By that time the dim light had brightened into full, blistering sun.

Feet from the rickety old shed, her body stopped abruptly. The morning sun beating down on her intensified the hot, muggy air, and sweat poured from her pores, an annoying trickle running down her face and into her eyes. There wasn't a damn thing she could do about it, but she could feel it.

Just like she could feel someone move to stand beside her. Because her gaze was fixed straight ahead, she wasn't able to see who it was, but she could feel a presence, hear the heavy mouth breathing.

Oh God, Two-Tooth.

Her hair moved. Was he stroking her hair? Helplessness washed over her and she wanted to scream out in horror. Especially as a hand slid across her cheek.

"I always thought you were real pretty."

Chills iced her veins. That was definitely Two-Tooth.

His breath sounded louder in her ear and she caught a whiff of the foul odor of it. What she wouldn't give to be able to cover her nose.

His hand brushed the hair away from her neck. "I bet you taste real good too." Something warm and wet pressed into her neck.

This was not good. Not at all. And she thought just being out of control of her limbs was torture.

While he continued to slobber on her neck, his hand moved down her chest to settle on her breast.

Please, please, please, body, she begged, *please respond.*

Nothing.

"Eugene!" Brigitte's voice cut through the on-her-knees-pleading she was mentally making. "You can play with your toy later. Right now, I got work for her to do."

"But, Ma!"

"Boy, don't make me come over there! Just leave her be for now. She'll be all yours later."

With a groan, Two-Tooth stepped away. And while Nichole released a huge internal sigh, she knew her relief was fleeting. Later would surely come too soon. She had to get control of her body before then. Had to.

She spent the entire day hauling heavy bags of something. Loose granules of some sort. She never actually saw the bags. They were plastic, had a funny odor, and weighed a ton. Without looking down, her body stooped to awkwardly pick them up and lumbered to a shed that reeked of an awful combination of cat piss and wet diapers.

It wasn't long before every inch of her skin was drenched in sweat. Her backed ached and her biceps burned, yet her body kept trudging on, unaware of the pains the work was causing.

All the while she worked, drums continued to pound in the background.

She caught sight of Daddy once, also performing some type of manual labor. Like before, he stared straight ahead through clouded, unfocused eyes. All she could think about was Claude Gautreaux and that…monster that roamed the swamp. And how he—and now she—must somehow be suffering the same curse. Though she hated knowing he was enduring the same torture, it still warmed her heart to see him alive. Sort of alive anyway.

And then her body simply stopped moving. Standing perfectly still in a thicket of marshy grass halfway between the shed and the house, she waited, terrified of what came next. Minutes ticked by. The drums faded and were replaced by the sound of low voices talking, the overwhelming buzz of cicadas, and the roar of her blood in her ears.

She felt like she was going to explode. She wanted to explode, to burst out of this prison of a body. Were people even looking for her? Did they know she was missing? And Julien... She'd been such a flake every time they'd been together—would he even realize she wasn't flaking this time? Would he know that she hadn't freaked out for the millionth time on him and simply taken off?

Why would he? She'd given him no reason to think she wasn't a complete spaz.

If she ever broke free from this curse, she'd be sure to let him know how much she did care for him. And how much she appreciated everything he'd done for her. And how she enjoyed every moment they'd spent together. And how she wanted more.

There had to be a way out. For her and for Daddy.

Heavy, thudding footsteps sounded behind her. Coupled with loud mouth-breathing, she knew it was Two-Tooth.

Oh. God.

She was about to be his plaything.

Her heart raced into action and with it her mind. *Run!* she screamed to her legs. *Run, you stupid fool!*

Of course nothing happened.

Two-Tooth was right behind her. "Thought I'd find you over here," he said, his mouth sounding like it was full of cotton.

His monkey paws ran down her sides and over her ass. She begged her head to flip back and head-butt him. When that didn't work, she willed her hands to clench into fists, which got her absolutely nowhere.

He leaned in to kiss her neck and then abruptly pulled back. "Ma! She stinks!"

Which Nichole certainly wouldn't deny—hours of hard labor and who knew how many hours in the swamp meant a special kind of odor covered her body. She was, however, shocked Two-Tooth noticed.

"So what?" Brigitte called back.

"It's gross!"

Who knew he had such a sensitive olfaction?

Whatever. She was definitely grateful for it.

"We'll clean her up after dinner," Brigitte said as she walked past Nichole. "You can play with her then."

"Okay," Two-Tooth said, defeated, and trudged after his mother toward the house.

Which left Nichole alone, spared for a little while longer, still standing completely immobile and staring blankly at the same spot through clouded vision. Insects droned on, animals cried out in the distance, birds fluttered overhead, objects splashed in the water, and the minutes ticked by while her mind silently screamed inside her prison.

She had to get out of there. Two-Tooth could return any minute and she didn't even want to think about what happened next. Her feet just had to move. *Move!* She'd get Daddy and swim back to Julien if that's what it took.

Just move. Please! Something. Anything...

But there was nothing but the endless spinning of her mind and the monotony of staring at the same worn spot on the shed with no idea what was happening around her besides what her ears revealed.

She would have chosen it over the heavy footsteps that clomped up behind her. Bracing for what came next, she tried to disappear into her mind, into thoughts and memories of anything but this situation. She thought about picturing the black painted door, about trying to disappear into the world of the dead, but before she could even consider if that was a good idea or not, cool mist showered her body, accompanied by the distinctive squeak of a spray bottle.

The fake scent of flowers wafted up to her nose as Two-Tooth came into view, the mist sprinkling down on her chest and stomach and legs. Was he spraying her with…air freshener? Was that his idea of cleaning her up?

She wasn't sure whether to be disgusted or repulsed or horrified. Maybe all of the above.

After her body was thoroughly saturated, Two-Tooth leaned in for a whiff. He could certainly use his own air freshener bath.

"That's better," he said, setting the bottle down before scooping her up and tossing her over his shoulder. "Let's go somewhere we can be alone."

Turning, he headed away from the house and toward the bayou. All Nichole could do was stare at his stained overalls and silently scream.

The boat motor whined loudly as Julien finally turned into the channel, like the annoying calls of a baby bird begging for food, or in this case, gas. Behind him, the sun was beginning to slip behind the trees, its warm orange glow a warning light of the pending darkness. It had taken him all afternoon to find the entrance, and that was only after he'd dug through the boat and found a map of the bayou.

Even then he'd struggled. It all looked the same out here. Water, some trees, some more water, more trees, a little moss, some snakes, the quickly disappearing eyeballs of stealthy alligators… It wasn't until he pulled his head out of his ass and his phone out of his pocket and checked the satellite map on the damn GPS that he figured out where the hell to turn.

By then the boat was running on fumes and his blood pressure had to be close to heart-exploding range. Dropping the motor into idle, he carefully navigated the narrow channel, painfully aware of every hum and splash.

Finding an obscure place to dock was now his first priority. The last thing he needed was another bullet hole in his body. Especially a lethal one. Besides Wendell, no one would even know if he were shot, bleeding to death, or worse, killed instantly. Rumors about his sudden disappearance would most likely involve Big Bubba.

And if he didn't do something, Nichole's disappearance would probably be lumped under the same excuse. There was no way in hell he was going to let her be their statistic.

The moment the blue GPS dot on his phone screen told him he was close, he turned off the motor and let momentum carry him to shore and in between two cypress trees drenched in moss—a perfect hiding space for the flat bottom boat. Rope in hand, he jumped onto marshy ground only slightly more solid than mud, quickly locating a sturdy, low-hanging limb before double knotting the rope around it.

The satellite image glowing back at him from his phone screen showed a little cleared spot that had to be the Villeres' place. If only he'd been paying more attention when Nichole brought him here, something might actually look familiar. As it was, he was relying on the phone's mapping software to get him there. He prayed the battery held out. Reception might be spotty, but he still had half a bar of battery life. It didn't look that far, and he just had to follow the channel, so he should be all right.

Checking that the gun was tucked securely into the waistband of his pants, he tossed his backpack over his shoulder and began walking. It took all of his attention to maneuver through dense brush and avoid being sucked into the numerous mud pits and pools of stagnant water.

The hike took longer than he thought. Even with the sun rapidly disappearing, the thick heat was turning him into a mess of sweat and more sweat. If he'd worn shorts he might have been cooler, but only if they came with a built-in air conditioner.

His legs would be a bloody mess though. Thorny bushes and shrubs that looked like half grown trees were everywhere, scratching like angry cats against his pants. A machete would have come in handy, and he would have brought one if it had been lying around. He pretty much brought everything else. Like a madman, he'd run around both his cabin and Nichole's, tossing anything that might be useful into his backpack. He might not know what to expect, but after last night and his previous run-in with his swamp cousins, he wanted to be prepared.

For a moment, he'd chastised himself for wasting so much time when Nichole could be in danger, but a nagging sensation wouldn't let him walk out the door until he'd overstuffed his backpack with what seemed like useless supplies—the Voodoo doll he'd made the night before, the box of salt, some water, the white candle and rosary beads from Nichole's failed *Beckoning*...

Grandmere had always insisted the little voice in a person's head that warned of danger was actually Loa, the spirits of Voodoo, whispering in their ear, and one should always take heed. He wasn't about to question that logic now.

Stinging sweat dripped in his eyes and he tried in vain to wipe it away with his equally sweaty arm. Stopping to crack the seal on one of a couple water bottles buried in his pack, he swallowed a few long gulps. He was contemplating showering in the lukewarm water when he heard what sounded like a man's voice coming from his right.

Like some sort of ninja, he dropped to a crouch, straining his senses to discern who it was and where the voice originated. Insects buzzing, frogs croaking, something splashing in the distance...all the noises of the swamp surrounded him, but no more voices. In spite of the racket, it seemed far too quiet.

At least three minutes went by before he heard the voice again, only this time it was a grunt. There was something sexual about it, something that made the hairs on his neck stand on end. And it was close.

He pulled away a web of thick prickly vines without caring they left tracks of blood on his forearm, revealing a scene that stole his breath.

Completely naked, Nichole stood motionless only fifteen feet from him. The shadowy outline of a man towered behind her, slobbering on her neck with his hands all over her breasts.

Holy fuck. Two-Tooth.

Rage sped through his veins, and it was all he could do not to leap from the bushes like a madman and rip that son of a bitch from limb to limb. He needed to wait, needed to think before acting. Who knew what that overgrown motherfucker had tucked in his pocket.

It was hard to stay calm with the throbbing in his temples. No doubt there were a few veins straining against his forehead and ready to burst. With gritted teeth, Julien delicately slipped off the backpack. Lifting the gun from his waistband, he checked the clip and then clicked off the safety, flinching when it clicked loudly. Luckily, Two-Tooth was more interested in groping Nichole's ass and not paying attention to his surroundings.

The fact that he was so engrossed in whatever creepy thing he was doing to Nichole just added fuel to Julien's rage, stoking the fire until it bubbled beneath his skin.

Still crouched down, he crept through thorny vines, a stagnant, murky puddle of water, and mud that smelled a lot like a pig farm until he had a clear view of Two-Tooth's wide back. As quietly as he could manage, he rose and tiptoed forward until he was close enough to jab the barrel of the gun right into Two-Tooth's fat head.

"You'd be smart to take your grubby hands off her." His voice was surprisingly calm given the horses galloping in his chest.

Two-Tooth jerked around and Nichole was pushed forward in the process. She looked like a mannequin as she fell to the ground, as stiff and straight as a board. Her arms didn't come out to break her fall, her body didn't crumple. She didn't react. At all. Even once she lay in the muck and mud.

He couldn't dwell on it. One of Two-Tooth's arms was swinging toward his head, sweeping around like the boom on a crane and almost as slowly. Julien ducked and spun away. Two-Tooth grunted as the expected blow missed and staggered forward.

Julien turned, preparing to pistol-whip him while he was vulnerable. But just as he tried to pivot, his foot stopped short, a pool of mud covering his shoe and holding his leg firmly in place. He yanked at it. The mud made a horrible sucking noise but held tight.

He'd managed to free a few inches when Two-Tooth hit him like a freight train. Knocked to the ground, his ankle twisted unnaturally as it was ripped from the mud. Pain shot up his leg just as a deafening shot went off.

He couldn't tell if the ringing in his ears was from the gunshot or his head hitting the ground. All the air in his lungs exploded out as Two-Tooth's massive body suffocated him. He gasped for breath, wishing he hadn't as his long-lost cousin's stench stung his nose.

Someone started wailing. For a moment, Julien had to make sure it wasn't him. Between the searing pain in his ankle, his throbbing head, and the giant trying to smother him, a wail wasn't out of the question.

It wasn't him though, it was Two-Tooth. Whimpering like a toddler with a scraped knee, the behemoth rolled to the side and Julien was finally able to gasp for air.

Clutching his leg, blood soaking his overalls, Two-Tooth howled, "I been shot! I been shot!"

With a cough and shake of his head to clear the stars from lack of oxygen, Julien rose. Pain shot through up his leg and through his spine, but he ignored it. He glanced briefly at Nichole, still motionless in the dirt. Fresh rage filled him as he turned to the other man.

"Get up," he snarled.

"You shot me!"

Julien point the gun at his head. "And if you don't get up, I'm going to shoot you again. This time I'll make a nice hole in your fucking head."

Anger wasn't an unfamiliar emotion for him, but the putrid hatred that coursed his veins was toxic. He could only remember one other time when he'd felt such seething—the brief, fleeting memories of being under Sanite Villere's control.

It was only that memory that kept him from putting another bullet in the asshole cowering on the ground before him.

"Remove one of your shoelaces," he said, keeping gun and gaze locked on him.

Two-Tooth obeyed, fumbling to remove the dirty white lace with blood-soaked fingers.

"Set it on the ground. Good. Now, turn around and put your hands behind your back."

With awkward, lumbering movements, Two-Tooth climbed to his knees and then turned away, jutting his arms behind him.

Tucking the gun into his waistband, Julien quickly lashed his wrists together with the shoelace. The little bastards were coming in handy—first to construct a Voodoo doll, then Nichole's salt necklace, now securing the village idiot.

"It's too tight. It hurts!"

"Shut up or I'll put a bullet in your other leg."

Once satisfied the restraint would hold, he rose and walked toward Nichole. Kneeling on the ground beside her, he whispered her name as he gently rolled her onto her back.

There was no way she was going to answer. Every hair on the back of his neck stood to attention now that he was close enough to really get a good look at her. Her naked, unprotected body was covered with scratches, mud, bruises, and insect bites—some so swollen they were bleeding. But it was her eyes that disturbed him the most. Cloudy, white, and unresponsive. Just like she described the missing old man she saw as a young girl in the swamp. Just like the rotting corpse he'd run into the other night.

"Nichole," he whispered again.

"It ain't gonna do you no good," Two-Tooth spouted. "She's ours now."

The rage returned with even more vehemence. Shoving himself to his feet, ignoring the burst of pain shooting up from his ankle, Julien marched over to the fat bastard still kneeling in the mud. He yanked the gun from his pants and shoved the barrel toward Two-Tooth's fat back. He wanted to pull the trigger so fucking bad his finger ached. Somehow he restrained himself.

"I'd like to say I'm sorry," he finally said. "But I'm not."

Using the handle of the gun, Julien cocked his hand back and clocked Two-Tooth in the back of the head with enough force that blood shot from his skull. With a grunt, he crumpled forward. It was the most satisfying sound Julien had heard in a while.

CHAPTER NINETEEN

Nichole hadn't moved two millimeters when he returned to her side. She continued to stare straight ahead with those unblinking, unfocused eyes. If he couldn't see the steady rise and fall of her chest, he'd swear she was dead. Carefully, he brushed the loose hair from her face. Her skin was warm, covered in a fine sheen of sweat beneath the filth and grime. He pressed his fingers to her neck. Her heart pulsed slow and steady beneath them. Her salt necklace was missing, but there was nothing he could do about that now.

Using the corner of his shirt as a rag, he gently wiped away the dirt smeared across her cheeks and brow. He caught a whiff of fake flowers, like someone had bathed her in Fabreeze.

God, if she would just blink. It was like the haze covering her eyes had trapped her soul and if he could clear it, she would return.

"I'm so sorry," he murmured. "I'll find a way to fix this."

Whatever "this" was.

It didn't matter. He *would* fix it.

"Let's get you the fuck out of here."

Scooping her into his arms, he rose, his leg wavering as his ankle protested loudly. Without adrenaline fueling him, it hurt like a bitch. Sprained, no doubt. Trudging back to the boat carrying one hundred and twenty-five pounds of dead weight was going to be fun.

"Suck it up, buttercup," he said to himself, shuffling over to the backpack and awkwardly stooping to pick it up while firmly keeping Nichole in his grasp.

There were several things he really needed to do: call the police and get some clothes on Nichole were at the top of his list. A tourniquet on Two-Tooth's leg probably wasn't a bad idea—since he really didn't want to get arrested for manslaughter—but the sun was quickly slipping below the horizon. Those things could wait until he got back to the boat and out into the main channel where it was a safe distance from gun-wielding meth dealers. He just prayed he had enough gas to make it. He'd also really like to get back to the boat before the swamp turned into a midnight maze. He only had minutes before that happened.

Time was not Julien's friend. Or it was possible the swamp was a black hole where time was sucked into some dark vortex. It certainly looked like a black hole, and the minutes of daylight he thought he had left only lasted for the first ten seconds of his journey back to the boat. At least that's how it seemed.

It didn't help that his ankle was on fire and every weed and shrub in the damn bayou seemed like it was out to trip him. And since he hadn't eaten all day, like the damn boat, he was running on fumes. He just had to push a little longer, a little harder. It couldn't be far.

Nichole remained catatonic and motionless the entire time. He avoided looking at her, hated seeing her staring lifelessly back at him. When she suddenly began kicking her legs, he almost dropped her.

He paused, glancing down at her for the first time since he'd started his trek. "Nichole? Can you hear me?"

Head tilted back, clouded eyes vacant and unfocused, it was clear she wasn't going to answer. Still, her legs kicked in rhythm, almost like she was marching.

Though faint, he thought he heard the sound of drumming in the distance. It took a moment for the sound to register. Between the fucking frogs and cicadas, all other noises were drowned out. Like a damn dog, he cocked his head in concentration to listen.

That was definitely a drum. And it wasn't coming from some hippie Burning Man drum circle. That was a Voodoo drum. He recognized the rhythm.

The volume seemed to increase, growing louder until it overrode the sounds of the bayou. Nichole's marching legs increased with each beat. As the drumming picked up, so did her movements until she was thrashing so violently in his arms he could barely keep his grip on her bare, sweat-slippery skin.

And she was strong as fuck. Far stronger than she should be. If he didn't set her down, he was going to drop her. Trying not to hurt her in the process, he eased her to the ground.

The moment she was free from his grasp, she mechanically lifted to her feet and began walking toward the sound of the drums.

Shit.

He hobble-jogged after her, wrapping his arms around her chest once he reached her. She thrashed against his grasp, twisting and fighting with inhuman force.

"Nichole!" he whispered harshly, tightening his grip. He didn't want to squeeze too hard. She was so much smaller than him and seemed so…fragile.

The drum tempo increased, and so did her attempts to escape. She finally succeeded, squirming from his arms and backhanding him across the face in the process.

He had to shake off the blow. Jesus, she was strong. And fast. How the hell was she covering so much wet, sodden, treacherous ground so quickly? Her methodical march was a lot more efficient than his half-ass attempt to run. It was like she was possessed.

Fuck. Fuck, fuck, fuck, fuck, fuck.

Could that be it? Could she be possessed?

That damn Voodoo drum got even louder, the rhythm so fast it was almost frenzied. And Nichole seemed to operate in time to the rhythm, her mechanical movements rapid as she glided effortlessly out of his sight.

He swore and took off after her again. His path wasn't nearly as effortless. Vines and tree branches grabbed at him with every step like hard, rough, spiky hands trying to hold him back. He fell twice, yanked to the ground by plants that he was sure were some sort of demon spawn.

It wasn't long before he had her in his sight again. The orange glow of a fire peeked through the vegetation, giving a clear view of her shadowy back. The drum grew louder with each sodden step, but it wasn't until she was within fifteen feet that he saw the source of the flames and the drum.

A bonfire roared in the center of a small clearing. He could make out four figures: one sat with a large conga drum between his knees, one appeared to be dancing, and two more stood motionless off to the side.

It wasn't much of a stretch to realize he'd stumbled onto the Swamp Villeres. Two-Tooth might be unconscious and restrained a good football field away, but Julien could only assume his parents were just as dangerous. And who knew about the other two.

Despite giving it everything he was worth, despite kicking his stride into super-sonic speed, he wasn't able to reach Nichole before she stepped into the clearing. Swearing once again under his breath, he slid to a stop, scrambling to gain traction so he could duck behind the nearest tree.

Patting the gun tucked in his waistband to make sure he hadn't dropped it in pursuit, he took a few deep breaths to try to steady his breathing and then cautiously peered around the tree.

Brigitte Villere must be the figure dancing next to the fire, while Norbert Villere played the drum. Both were dressed in loose white clothing, though what Brigitte wore could hardly be described as clothing. More like an open robe. Her breasts were bared and she held a large black snake above her head, her skin dripping with moisture, her hips undulating back and forth ferociously.

Both the rhythm and her movements were hypnotic. In fact, the other two figures appeared, like Nichole, to be in a trance.

The flickering flame cast shadows on their faces, and Julien had to squint to get a better look, craning his body as far forward as his cover safely allowed. He was pretty sure he knew what he'd find, but he had to make sure, had to confirm his suspicions.

It was as he suspected—and feared. One of the static figures was the old man from the swamp, a man Julien could only assume was Claude Gautreaux. His clouded eyes stared straight ahead. The same dead stare haunting Nichole's face. A burst of firelight suddenly illuminated the old man's face, sending icy shivers down Julien's spine. A small slab of skin drooped from Claude's cheek, peeling away like bark on an aspen tree to reveal the pink muscle beneath.

Julien forced himself to look away and toward the other figure. He'd seen enough pictures to immediately recognize Nichole's father, Robert Montoya. His eyes were the same as hers and Claude's, his posture as rigid and still as the other two. Luckily, his flesh looked intact.

The drum rhythm abruptly shifted from frenzied to a slow, steady beat. Brigitte continued to dance, the snake in her hands, her body writhing and twisting. The White Eyes, as Nichole had called them, stirred to life.

Like robots, they marched in unison toward a large, haphazardly stacked woodpile. With machine-like steadiness, they began splitting the wood in assembly-line fashion. Claude would balance a log on the chopping block, Robert would split it, and Nichole would stack it neatly off to the side. Balance, chop, stack. Repeat. Balance, chop, stack.

He was reminded of the figures in a cuckoo clock. The way every movement seemed timed to the steady beat of the drum, as if the rhythm controlled their every move...

Of course! He knew exactly what was wrong with Nichole and her father! Shay had been right after all. They were Zonbis. Not the zombies of horror novels, though Claude's peeling skin might indicate otherwise, but Voodoo Zonbis.

Turning away from the scene, Julien leaned wearily against the tree. He knew little about Zonbis. It just wasn't an aspect of the religion he'd studied. The only things he knew were academic in nature. Nothing in his research prepared him for this. Nothing.

What he did know didn't bode well for Nichole or her father. From his understanding, Zonbis were souls harvested by a Voodoo sorcerer, a Boko, after they suffered an unnatural death. Once the souls were captured, the Boko could control the bodies, turning them into slaves.

But Nichole wasn't dead. She couldn't be. She wasn't. He'd felt her heartbeat.

Right?

Freeing Zonbis might be well beyond his expertise, but he knew someone who could help.

Grandmere would have been ideal, but since she was no longer with them, his mother would have to do.

Crouching down, he crept away from the bonfire and into the inky bayou darkness. The wildlife singing their nightly chorus should be enough to drown out any noise he might make, but he needed to get far enough away that the light of his cell phone wasn't visible. He just prayed he had enough battery and a strong enough signal to make the phone call.

He waited until the fire was barely a dim flicker in the background before pulling out his phone. One bar, both for signal and battery. It was well after nine, so Delia Villere should be home. It was too early for a séance and late enough that the Jackson Square crowd had died down. Hopefully she'd actually answer. It wasn't uncommon for her to have either misplaced her phone or let the battery die.

His heart quit beating while he dialed. When the phone actually rang instead of going straight to voicemail, it beat once. When his mother actually answered, the organ picked up the slack.

"Thank God," he breathed.

"Who is this?"

Didn't she have his number programmed into her phone?

"It's Julien." He tried not to sound annoyed, but his voice came out dry and flat. Not that she picked up on it.

"Oh, Julien. Good. Can you pick up some toilet paper while you're out?"

He pulled the phone back to give it an incredulous stare. "No," he said into the receiver.

Her sigh was audible even over the phone. It bordered on a groan. "This is so typical of you. Fine, I'll have Xavier do it."

If he could have reached through the phone to throttle her he would have. "Mom, I'm not even in New Orleans."

"What? Yes you are. I saw you this morning. Wait...didn't I?"

"No. I'm nowhere near the city."

"Huh. That's so odd..."

"Look," he cut off her trailing sentence. "I really need your help. It's urgent."

"Well, hurry up because I'm busy and now I have to go get toilet paper. I can't seem to find your brother. I don't know where he keeps running off to. Ever since Lottie moved in... Though he is still having a hard time since Grandmere passed—"

"Mom! Focus. Please. This is really important."

"What do you need, Julien?"

"What do you know about Voodoo Zonbis? Specifically, how do you free them? Can the curse be reversed?"

"Why?" There was more than a hint of suspicion in her voice.

"I just need to know. Someone close to me is being held captive."

"Here in New Orleans?"

Holy shit. His head was going to fucking explode. He wanted to scream into the phone, but instead took a deep breath and said through gritted teeth, "I'm. Not. In. New. Orleans."

"Oh. Right. I swear I saw you this morning..."

"Mom! Zonbis! How do you free them?"

"Hmm. Well, you have sever the connection."
"What connection?"
"The connection between the Voodoo priest and the Zonbis. The Zonbi's free will has been stolen from them and has to be kept somewhere, usually in a vessel of some sort, like a bottle or something. That's how the Boko controls them. Are these living Zonbis or dead Zonbis?"

"Um...both. I think. Let's just focus on the live Zonbis."

"Well, living may or may not apply. Even if they were alive when they became a Zonbi, that doesn't mean they're still alive."

"For argument's sake, let's just pretend they're still alive. How do I sever the connection? What happens after?"

"Find the vessel and destroy it. That's the first step for sure. You may have to appeal to Baron Samedi for help—he controls Zonbis, of course—but otherwise that should be all it takes. If the Zonbis are still alive, they will regain control of their bodies. If not..."

He felt his stomach drop to his shoes. "What?"

"Well, honey, they're dead. The Loa have been keeping them animated. They'll just...disintegrate. Depending on how long they've been dead, of course."

He was pretty sure he'd fucking lose it if he saw Nichole disintegrate. It was a risk he needed to take.

His phone beeped at him, warning of a low battery.

"Okay, thanks, Mom. I really appreciate everything."

"No problem. Hey, bring home toilet paper, will you?"

He didn't bother answering. The phone disappeared back into his pocket and he began the wet journey back to the fire circle.

CHAPTER TWENTY

Robert, Nichole, and Claude were still methodically stacking wood when Julien reached the edge of the circle, the slow and steady drum rhythm matching their purposeful movements.

Eyes closed, Norbert pounded relentlessly on the goblet drum, an ill-fitting top hat balanced on his head, swaying with every downbeat. Now that Julien was closer he could see that each of his fingers were taped and blood seeped at the edges.

Brigitte still danced, but her movements were now more like a stoner at a jam band concert. Gaze toward the ground, snake draped across her neck, she swayed like the top hat. Back and forth, back and forth, back and forth.

He grimaced as the snake twisted in her hand. He hated snakes. Had all his life. It didn't matter that the snake was a prominent symbol in Voodoo, often representing the most powerful Loa, Damballah. He still hated them.

It might anger the spirits, but the moment the chance presented itself, he was going to kill that thing. First things first, he needed to take care of that drum. It was obvious that the rhythm was controlling the Zonbi slaves. Nichole hadn't tried to move until it started, so the first thing he was going to do was silence it.

Keeping low to the ground, he duck-walked around the perimeter of the clearing, stopping when he was directly behind Norbert. Careful not to make a sound, he eased the gun from his waistband as he slowly rose and crept toward him. Clasping the barrel, he drove the grip into the back of Norb's head.

Sounds of the bayou overtook the clearing as the drumming came to an abrupt stop. Norbert slumped to the side like a sack of dog food. Who knew a gun handle would end up being the weapon of choice? Thank goodness for the countless action movies he'd watched over the years. Julien had only handled a gun a few times in his life. Now he was pistol-whipping people like an expert.

Nichole, Robert, and Claude also abruptly stopped. Nichole and Claude happened to be in standing positions and were able to stay upright. Robert wasn't so lucky. In the middle arc of an axe swing when his body halted, momentum carried him forward and he face-planted the ground, hard. Luckily, he missed anything more solid, like the stump or his axe, or even the piece of wood waiting to meet the axe blade, or it might have been his head that split.

Checking to see if he was all right was out of the question. The most inhuman shriek cut through the din of the swamp, piercing his eardrums like nails on a chalkboard, or a group of thirteen-year-old girls at the mall. From the corner of his eyes, he spotted a flash of white and a pair of crazed eyes. He spun just in time to avoid being blindsided by Brigitte Villere, scooting away from her and into the center of the circle.

Undeterred, she changed course in a few jerking steps and charged toward him again. Still grasping the snake in flailing arms stretched high about her head, her bare breasts flapped wildly beneath her open robe.

Except for the writhing serpent clutched in her hands, nothing about her attempted attack should have frightened him. Her eyes, though... He'd seen that expression in his nightmares. Felt that level of hatred deep in his soul from a source outside of himself. It reeked of the toxic air filled with putrid emotions that had haunted his dreams over and over again since last spring.

Facing Brigitte wasn't an issue. Facing Sanite was.

It was a hesitation tossed aside when the snake was inches from his face. Snapping out of his shocked daze, he juked just as she lunged for him. Unable to stop her forward movement, she careened toward the fire.

He was able to catch her before things ended worse than they were by grabbing the back of what little fabric covered her body. He jerked her back to safety, the dirty white cotton ripping but holding long enough for him to secure her in a choke hold.

The snake wasn't so lucky. Torn from her grasp by physics, it flew into the middle of the three-foot tall bonfire. Julien was pretty sure it hissed the entire way. That was quite possibly just the fire, but he certainly didn't feel any remorse for the beast.

Like the snake that recently met its demise, Brigitte squirmed and writhed, struggling against his grip, slapping futiley at the arm around her neck. Unlike Nichole, he wasn't too concerned with hurting her, so he squeezed with everything he had.

"Quit fighting," he snapped. "It won't hurt my feelings if you pass out."

His words fell on deaf ears. She screeched, her arms swinging around wildly as she attempted to hit his face or maybe claw out his eyes. When that didn't work, she stamped her bare feet until one came in contact with his toes.

Not that it mattered. It certainly didn't hurt, but it did piss him off. He increased the pressure on her neck until she began making strangled choking noises. Her hands flew back to his arm, clawing at the flesh. He took the break in her squirming to pin one of her arms, and then after releasing her neck, the other.

She immediately let out a blood-curdling scream.
"Jesus. Shut up."

Keeping her arms tightly pinned behind her back, he marched her away from the fire and toward Norbert, still out cold. Judging from the blood dribbling down his skull, it would probably be a while before he woke.

Julien forced her to sit beside Norbert. Still keeping her arms tightly contained and probably painfully squeezed behind (not that he cared much), he awkwardly removed his belt. First Two-Tooth's shoelace and now his belt. What he wouldn't give for some fucking rope.

Looping the leather around her arms and through the buckle, he pulled tight, feeling just a little sadist satisfaction when she squealed. He then threaded the belt around Norbert's closest arm, scooped up the other one hanging limply at his side, and somehow managed to get the belt around both and then secured through the clasp.

A tree or something else secure would have been nice, but at this point Norbert was pretty much a two-hundred pound paperweight, so he felt pretty confident Brigitte wasn't going anywhere. He would knock her out, but actually felt a little weird about just cold-cocking a woman. Maybe there actually was a little chivalry in him after all.

Satisfied his long-lost cousins were contained, he moved to check on the victims. First he rolled Robert Montoya onto his back, checking him over quickly to make sure nothing looked too damaged. He was in worse shape than Nichole—completely nicked up and covered in bug bites from head to toe. He also smelled a bit like Bourbon Street. Actually, a little worse than Bourbon Street.

His face was gaunt, the hollows below his milky eyes as pronounced as his protruding cheekbones. All the pictures Julien had seen in Nichole's cabin showed a healthy, robust man, not this walking skeleton. It looked like he hadn't eaten in days, which seemed likely.

Scared of what he might find, Julien hesitantly placed the tips of his fingers against Robert's neck, breathing a sigh of relief when the skin was warm and there was a pulse.

Not that he knew for sure that meant Robert was alive, but the opposite definitely meant he wasn't. If his emaciated appearance was any indication, he wasn't going to last much longer.

He moved his attention to Nichole, skipping Claude as he passed. Judging from the old man's peeling skin and rotten smell, a pulse would have actually been even more of a curse.

Thankfully Nichole didn't look any worse than she had earlier, but she didn't look any better either. She may no longer be controlled by that fucking drum, but she was no closer to being freed from the Zonbi spell either.

He needed to find that vessel and fast.

"It don't matter what you do," Brigitte said behind him. "She's ours now."

Repeating Two-Tooth's words was a mistake. His blood leapt to a boil, cooking violently beneath his skin. Whipping the gun from his waistband, he marched toward her, pointing the weapon directly at her face. If she was fazed it didn't show.

"Tell me how to free them!" he demanded.

She flashed a partially toothed grin. "Ain't nothin' you can do, boy. It's Voodoo. Only one of us can control them. And you ain't one of us."

"I think you missed the fucking memo," he said through gritted teeth. "And the gun pointed at your head."

"You won't pull the trigger. You ain't got the balls."

Man if that didn't make him want to prove her wrong. But she was right. He could be a selfish dick, he was seething with rage, and he seemed pretty good at the pistol-whipping, but there was no way he could blow someone's head off in cold blood. Hell, as much as he wanted to kill that snake, if it hadn't flown into the fire, he probably would have just let it go.

"'Sides, I already told you, you got to be Voodoo to do anything here."

"And I said you missed the memo. We haven't been introduced, but I'm Julien Villere. Apparently, we're long-lost cousins, descendants of the same Villere line. Sanite and Laurent Villere. I'm sure you've heard of your great-great-great-great grandmother, right?"

Her eyes went wide.

"So you're going to free my friends."

What started as a low chuckle quickly escalated to a crazed laugh, which she abruptly stopped and then spit on the ground. "No. She don't want them freed."

His shoulders were so tense and tight it felt like they might snap when he shrugged it off. "Fine," he said tightly. "I'll just do it myself. Don't expect any Christmas presents, cuz. Ever. And I'm not visiting you in jail either."

She spit on the ground again. "You'll never free them! Never! They belong to us!"

"We'll see about that." He scanned the Villeres and the area around them for anything that might work as a vessel for lost souls. There wasn't anything.

"What are you looking for?"

"None of your damn business."

Maybe Norbert had something in his pockets. He reached forward to pat him down.

"What are you doing? Get away from him."

"Shut up." After coming up empty on the first pocket, he moved to the second, the one next to Brigitte.

As soon as he got close, she lunged at him, teeth bared. He jerked back. "What the fuck is wrong with you?"

"Don't touch him."

"You already said that and I think I remember telling you to shut up." Pressing one hand against her shoulder to keep her shoved back, he quickly searched Norbert's other pocket. Again, nothing. No bottles, flasks, pill cases, Altoid tins... All he found out was some lint and a crumpled up receipt.

"Fuck," he said, stepping back.

"You won't find it," Brigitte said smugly.

"Shut it." Julien scanned the area again. There had to be something. His mother might be a flake, but he didn't doubt her on this. It made sense they would keep the vessel close, but maybe he needed to expand the search area. He had to be missing something.

Stepping back to get a better look, he stumbled over Norbert's drum. Pausing, he stared at it. There wasn't anything special about it, just a run of the mill conga drum. They sold similar ones at the Voodoo shop.

Something made him linger. Really, there wasn't anything unusual about the drum—except that it had been controlling Nichole and her father. He knew drums were a huge part of Voodoo rituals, but could it be more than that? It *was* a vessel of sorts.

Only one way to find out.

"What are you doing?" Brigitte asked again. There was something about her voice...

He scooped up the drum.

"Put that down!" There was no mistaking the urgency in her tone. She didn't want him anywhere near this drum. Which was exactly why he should be interested in it.

He glanced at her. "You aren't very bright, are you? Too many years of inbreeding, eh?" Drum in hand, he turned toward the fire.

"What are you doing?" Brigitte screeched behind him. "Stop! Don't go any further!"

"Didn't I tell you to shut-up?" Julien tossed the remark over his shoulder at the same time he tossed the drum into the fire.

All at once the entire world seemed to fall apart. The drum exploded in a burst of sparks and splintered wood, Brigitte started screaming like a banshee, and the fire shot up a good thirty feet, bathing the small clearing in light.

Covering his face with his arm, he spun away, knees hitting the ground as he ducked. He could feel shrapnel hit his back and was thankful Nichole had been frozen in place with her back to the fire. With those unblinking eyes, being bombarded with shards of wood could be a bad deal. Hopefully Robert was far enough away to avoid being hit.

"Now you've done it!" Brigitte screamed. "You're going to be sorry! We won't forget this!"

Ignoring her, he rose, brushing shards of drum and ash from his clothes. All his body parts felt intact. When Brigitte began stamping her feet in rhythm he also ignored her. She muttered something soft and low in time with the foot stamps. He had better things to worry about than what she was chanting. He started to turn for Nichole and the others, to check and see how they fared when her singsong words began to register.

"Mambo Sanite, Mambo Sanite, your children are calling. Mambo Sanite, Mambo Sanite, your children need you." She repeated the verse, more loudly this time. "Mambo Sanite, Mambo Sanite, your children are calling. Mambo Sanite, Mambo Sanite, your children need you."

Shit. This might be bad.

When she started the verse for the third time, now nearly shouting, he knew he needed to do something.

"Jesus! Would you put a sock in it already! In fact..." With heavy footsteps, he marched the few feet to her. Tearing a corner of fabric from her "dress," he waded it up, and then used one hand he force her mouth open. She tried to jerk away, but he increased the pressure on her jaw until she had no choice but to open wide. He shoved the fabric into her mouth then ripped off another strip and used it to tie the gag.

Why hadn't he thought of gagging her in the first place?

With Brigitte finally quiet, he was able to hear soft moaning coming from the other side of the circle. Heart in his throat, he turned to see the source.

It was Robert Montoya. Rolling gently on the ground, he appeared to be trying to rise. Could it have worked? Was the drum the vessel after all?

Claude was nowhere to be seen, but a pile of bones and flesh sat where he'd stood only moments earlier. And Nichole... She turned toward him with halting steps. Her expression might have been dazed, shocked even, and her skin drained of color, but it was her! Normal dark, beautiful eyes and all!

CHAPTER TWENTY-ONE

Everything in her body hurt. Every muscle, every inch of skin, every organ. Even each individual hair follicle was on fire with pain. And nothing seemed to work right. But at least things worked! And even if every step felt like she was walking on needles, at least she was walking.

Tears filled her eyes and streamed down her cheeks. Partly in response to the desert in her eyes, partly from pain, but mostly out of joy.

Daddy. She had to get to him.

And Julien. Where was Julien?

Turning toward the heat of the fire at her back gave her at least one of her wishes. Julien was rushing toward her. Her heart swelled at the sight of him. The last day may have been shrouded in fog, but with clarity she remembered him rescuing her from Two-Tooth and the affectionate way he'd cleaned the dirt from her face. The expression on his handsome face was filled with nothing but relief, happiness, and love. All for her.

Besides Daddy, she'd never been so happy to see someone.

He pulled her into a quick, but gentle embrace. "God," he whispered into her hair. "I thought I'd lost you." Kissing her forehead, he pulled back. "You are back, right?"

She nodded, even that tiny gesture painful. It felt like her brain was sloshing around in her skull.

"Good. C'mon, let's get you to your father."

Gratitude overfilled her heart. He knew exactly what she needed. It wasn't the first time either. With the exception of their initial meeting, he'd been able to read her from the beginning, knowing just what she needed and then stepping in to help. Even if she didn't recognize or want it at first.

"Here." Stripping off his shirt, he slipped it over her head, easing her arms through the sleeves like an infant.

Once again, gratitude made her heart feel like it was going to burst. She'd forgotten she was naked. Maybe it should be a small detail at this point, but reuniting with Daddy in a complete state of undress was hardly ideal. Of course Julien would protect her from any embarrassment, no matter how insignificant.

"Thank you." Her voice was a painful, hoarse whisper, her throat like raw wood.

He touched her chin. "Of course."

Once she was sufficiently decent, he helped her kneel by her father's side and then ease him up into a sitting position. Despite the wrenching twisting her guts at his appearance, the tears streaming down her cheeks felt good. Like a cleansing bath for her eyes and soul.

Julien lingered only for a moment, seeming to verify they were stable before rising and stepping away, pulling a phone from his pocket.

She wanted to express how grateful she was for him, how much he meant to her, how she wanted him in her life, but now wasn't the time. She had to focus on Daddy.

He looked far worse than even she felt. Eyes that had been clouded over were now nearly solid red they looked so irritated. He was thin to the point of starvation, skin filthy and raw, like it had been chewed on and spit out. But the worst part of all was the haunted look on his face. Judging from her own limited experience, she could only imagine the torture he must have gone through.

"Oh, Daddy," she cried, doing her best imitation of *throwing* her arms around his neck since they responded sluggishly instead of enthusiastically.

"Nikki." His voice was barely a hoarse whisper, more like a raspy breath of escaping air. She felt his arm try to raise and fail. She hugged him tighter.

"I knew you weren't dead. They all thought—but I knew. I'm so glad I found you!"

"Me too, baby. Me too."

She gripped him tighter, refusing to let go for even a second, even as the fire seemed to erupt behind her.

Keeping Nichole and her father in his peripheral vision, Julien powered on his phone. There wasn't much juice left, the battery bar red and ominous looking, like it was warning of bad things to come. At least he had some semblance of a signal. Hopefully it would be enough to get one final call in.

"911, what's your emergency?"

"Yeah, I'm out at the Villeres' place out on Bayou Grisé. I need whatever emergency services you can send. Police, a medic, maybe an ambulance—assuming there's a boat type—we're probably good on the fire truck, though."

"Is someone hurt?"

"Yes. At least one needs to be treated for exposure." He paused. Two-Tooth should probably get a mention. "And I got one that's been sho—" The phone beeped obnoxiously in his ear, effectively cutting off his sentence.

He glanced at it. The battery was about to give up. Something in his gut nagged at him, sending unease throughout his body. There wasn't a hint of breeze, but the flames danced left then right, smoke swirling through the clearing in a spiraling vortex. They then died down to barely more than embers, sending the clearing into darkness. Every hair on his body jumped to attention. Oh shit.

"Sir?" the faint voice of the operator squeaked from his phone. "Sir, are you there?"

Besides the measly glow from the few embers in the fire pit, his phone was the only source of light in the clearing. He put it to his ear, swallowing against the rising tension in his throat. "Yeah, I'm here—" Another obnoxious beep sounded and the screen went black.

Shit squared.

In the faint glow from what was left of the fire, he could see Nichole still embracing her father. He needed to be near them. He wasn't sure what the fuck was happening, but he didn't want to be too far away.

He started back toward them when without warning the fire burst up, exploding at least thirty feet into the night sky, flames tickling the canopy above. Slowly they eased down, twisting and turning until they loosely formed the shape of a woman.

Shit, shit, shit.

Her presence was undeniable. Hatred filled the air like thick fog, saturating everything it touched. It seemed to penetrate his skin, seeping into his blood. Sanite.

Rage immediately swept through him as every injustice he'd ever experienced was brought to the surface.

His father leaving, abandoning him when Julien needed him most. Not just abandoning, but blaming him for the shitty way his life had turned out.

"If I didn't have you and your brother and your crazy ass mother dragging me down, things would be different. I would be different. Better. Not broke-ass in this filthy city with two worthless kids."

The words, slurred in a drunken rage one night, had been cut into Julien's memory with jagged glass, fueling years of angst and drug and alcohol abuse. Even the beatings Julien had endured at his father's hand weren't as painful. And it didn't matter if the man had been horrible, a boy needs his father. Julien needed him.

And then fucking Xavier. Always so perfect. Grandmere's favorite. Mom's favorite. Maybe Julien hadn't reacted well when his dad left, but he was still the oldest. He should have become the man of the house. But no, that punk-ass Xavier had to step in and shove Julien aside in his "Xavier knows best" routine.

Damn it, he just wanted to punch something. Someone, anyone.

He whipped around to a wide-eyed Brigitte. Nostrils flared, breath heaving in and out of lungs, he could feel a snarl curling up his top lip. He felt like he could easily wring her neck.

"Not them!" a voice slammed into brain. *"Them..."*

His head turned toward Robert and Nichole. And then his body. And then his feet began slowly moving. He could feel the clenching of his fists, balled and ready to strike. It was all disconnected though, like he was watching himself from some distance away.

The hatred increased with every step, rising up through the ground and into his veins. Hatred directed and the father and daughter embraced before him. How dare they get their happy ending? Julien never got one. His father was God knew where right now. He should be the one in Nichole's arms. He saved her.

Less than five feet of dirt and mud separated him from the Montoyas. Nichole glanced at him, fear and doubt all over her face.

"Julien? What's wrong?"

Her voice sounded like she'd gargled broken glass. He paused, confusion making his brain foggy.

This was exactly the scene he desired—Nichole reunited with her father. This was why he was here. He wasn't jealous of their reunion. It's what he wanted all along because ultimately, Nichole's happiness was all that mattered.

"No," the voice whispered in the back of his head. *"She should be praising you, not him. He did nothing but get her into this mess."*

Julien felt his eyebrows push together. Was that how he felt? The emotions *seemed* to be his. Was he really that petty?

"Julien?" Nichole's voice cut through his confusion.

Fuck no, those weren't his feelings. He knew what this was, and he wasn't going to fall under Sanite's spell again.

Physically shaking the hatred from his body, he spun and scrambled for the backpack. He knew what he had to do now. Sanite needed to go. Permanently.

Brigitte's chant for Sanite should have been warning enough. Why wouldn't her hand be in this? Why hadn't he seen it?

He ripped through the sack, pulling out the Voodoo doll and the carton of salt. The whimsical image of a girl with an umbrella seemed so out of place right now. He wasn't exactly sure what he'd do with them, but he'd think of something.

Mom had said to summon Baron Samedi, so that's just what he'd do. As luck would have it, he even had a couple offerings, items he liked to keep on hand for personal emergencies: a pack of smokes and a flask filled with bourbon. The Baron preferred rum, but Beam would have to do.

Grabbing a fallen branch at the edge of the cleared circle before returning to the center, he closed his eyes for a moment to make a mental roadmap of Samedi's vévé. Once satisfied he remembered it correctly, he carefully began drawing the symbol in the dirt and mud. More intricate than many vévés, he started with the outline of the cross, quickly progressing to the raised platform it stood on.

The fire roared before him, hissing and popping with threatening violence. He ignored it. Just like he ignored Sanite's voice when she tried to break back into his head.

He had just started drawing one of the coffins flanking the cross when Nichole's startled, strained scream jerked his attention away. She was struggling to rise, tugging in vain at her father as she stared in horror at a spot across the circle. He spun his gaze that direction and had to silence his own horrified outburst.

The rotten *thing* he'd run into the other night was stumbling, dragging, heaving its flesh-dripping body directly toward Nichole.

Abandoning the mud sketch and tossing the stick aside, he ran for them, quickly helping Nichole, and then Robert, to their feet. He gently tried to usher them out of the path of the Zonbi without much success. Nichole took a few staggering steps but Robert simply collapsed back onto the ground.

He stooped to retrieve the fallen man, carefully but quickly righting him. Robert swayed uneasily and Julien immediately knew there was no way he could walk three feet, let alone run from a Zonbi.

"Julien!" Nichole's voice, quiet and hoarse as it was, was a five-alarm siren in his ears.

He jerked his attention around. The corpse was barely five feet away.

Slinging one arm around Robert and hoisting him up like a toddler, Julien somehow managed to twist around, scoop up Nichole in his other arm and bolt to the other side of his abandoned véve drawing just as the Zonbi stagger-dragged his sinewy legs inches from where they'd been standing.

Shay had said the zombies weren't aggressive, but that wasn't what Julien saw. Nichole, Robert, and the late Claude had been under Brigitte and Norbert's control, only able to do their bidding. Julien couldn't be sure, but it was only logical this Zonbi—if he had to guess, the unfortunate late, late, late, Pascal Grisé—was under Sanite's control. And with her running the show, he had to assume Pascal was dangerous.

He was planning his escape route from the clearing when his ankle unexpectedly gave out, searing pain shooting up his leg. He must have stepped on it wrong, aggravating the earlier injury.

He tumbled to the ground, Nichole and Robert collapsing with him. There was no need to look, the stench told him the Zonbi was closing the gap his shuffle had granted.

Think, Julien. Think!

Ignoring the stabbing protesting of his ankle, he pushed to his feet and turned to face the corpse. It was coming fast, faster than those rotten legs should allow.

If Sanite was controlling it, Julien knew the only way to stop it would be to stop her. But to do that, he needed Baron Samedi's help. And to get the Baron's help, he needed time.

Bracing himself, he coiled back. Exploding off his good leg, he lunged forward. Using his hands as braces, he shoved as hard as he could. His hands sank into something wet and mushy, but it worked, and the Zonbi flew backward, the impact separating it from its left foot.

Swallowing against the bile singeing the back of his throat and without looking at whatever disgustingness coated them, he wiped his hands on his pants.

Despite missing a foot, the Zonbi clumsily began to rise. With only a few seconds to spare, Julien hobbled for the salt container lying on the ground next to the half-drawn vévé . A protective circle probably wouldn't work against the Zonbi since he wasn't technically a ghost, but Julien knew who was. And he had an idea how he might be able to gain a few more precious seconds. He didn't think it would stop her, but it might weaken her just enough.

Like when he threw the drum into the fire, flames surged high into the sky when the salt container landed in it, screaming and hissing in protest, sending embers and sparks everywhere. And then, just as quickly, the fire recessed to coals.

Julien glanced briefly over his shoulder to verify his theory had worked. The Zonbi had stopped in its tracks. Wasting no more time, he returned to the vévé, finishing the first coffin and then rapidly drawing the second.

The fire was already regaining strength. Two small flames licking eagerly at the air quickly became three, then four, then merging into one larger fire. He drew faster, filling in the vévé details. When he was satisfied it bore enough resemblance to the symbol, he pulled out his flask, took a quick swig, and then set it and the half-smoked pack of cigarettes at the base of the dirt drawing.

Clapping his hands in rhythm and keeping the Zonbi in his peripheral, he stepped back and began his chant. "Baron, my Baron, Samedi my king, I leave you this offering, your help I beseech."

The fire flared up, a low hissing rising up from the middle. He sped up the rhythm, clapping his hands loudly together and repeating the chant.

That definitely got Sanite's attention. The fire raged to life, blasting him with a wave of heat just as he was blasted by the stench of rotten flesh. The Zonbi was feet away, hobbling even more awkwardly on its peg leg.

Almost as awkwardly, Julien limped away from its rotten grasp, pain scorching every step. "Baron...my Baron...Samedi my king, I leave you this offering, your help—"

The flames seemed to reach for him, interrupting the chant and strangling him with their heat. Smoke filled his lungs, choking out his breath as heat seared his flesh. Suddenly frozen in place, he couldn't seem to move, his legs refusing to comply, his voice just as frozen in his throat.

The Zonbi closed in, reaching for him with half-fleshed fingers. He would have ducked, would have shoved the monster away, but nothing responded. Bony fingers dug into his flesh as he was pushed to the ground. The stench stung his eyes just as sharply as the smoke, and his body, unwilling to respond any other way, began to retch as the rotten corpse descended upon him.

Well, this was it. Never in a million years did he expect to go out like this—a gruesome scene in some horror movie. He only hoped his pending "death by zombie" would grant Nichole and Robert the chance to escape.

The creature's gaping maw and dangling, clouded over eye were millimeters from contact when unexpectedly it seemed to explode above him. The head flew toward the fire, scattering bits of flesh everywhere as what was left of its body crumpled on top of him.

When the Zonbi skull reached the fire, the flames reacted, coiling back and hissing in protest. At that moment, he regained control of his limbs. With disgust and just a little bit of bile, he shoved the body aside. Above him stood Nichole, leaning wearily on the splitting axe and breathing like she'd just finished climbing Mount Everest.

"Hurry," she rasped.

Nodding, he began the arduous task of rising, pain spiking with every movement. His ankle, his arm, his neck—which felt warm and wet. "Baron, my Baron," he panted, rolling to his side, "Samedi, my king…" He struggled to his knees. "…I leave you this offering…" Hands braced on his thighs, he rose shakily to his feet. "…your help I beseech!"

The fire flickered as wind swirled through the clearing. Smoke and embers twisted together in a haze hovering over the vévé even as the flames recoiled further. A smoky image of Baron Samedi formed in the haze—wearing a top hat, tuxedo, and smoking a cigar between his skeleton teeth. With a toothy grin, he stooped and picked up the flask, removing the cigar and pouring the liquor into his open mouth. The amber liquid dribbled through his skeleton ribs and into the dirt. He then lit one of the cigarettes off the butt of his cigar. Wispy tendrils of smoke drifted from it as he inhaled, joining the smoke from the fire forming his body.

Carrying the flask and cigarettes with him, he floated toward Julien, giving Nichole a once over as he passed. Known for being a crude womanizer, Julien was half-surprised the apparition didn't smack her on the ass.

Samedi stopped before him, holding the flask and cigarettes out. Julien took them cautiously, wondering if they were somehow unsatisfactory. When he took the objects, the Baron lifted the Voodoo doll from Julien's pocket and presented it as well, putting the cigar back into his mouth and nodding toward the doll.

And suddenly Julien knew exactly what he needed to do.

As soon as he accepted the doll, Samedi slowly disintegrated, disappearing in a scattering of ash. Immediately the fire began regaining strength. Sanite didn't waste any time, did she?

Julien turned to Nichole. "I'm going to need your, and your father's help," he told her.

"Of course. Anything."

He'd love to be able to properly thank her for the help she'd already given him, but there wasn't time now. Hobble-jogging over to Robert, still helpless on the ground, he lifted him up and limped back over to Nichole. It was the one moment he was thankful for the older man's drastic weight loss. With his ankle being a bitch and all the other injuries he seemed to have sustained, carrying a normal Robert would have a greater struggle than it already was.

He set the older man down next to Nichole. "Take his hand. We need the power of three for this."

She complied. Julien linked his arm through Robert's to complete their connection as well as help keep him steady.

Luckily, Julien's body was leaking blood from enough places that he was able to wipe a little on the Voodoo doll before holding it at the center of their semi-circle. From the corner of his eye, he saw the headless corpse begin to rise. The fire was quickly building, black smoke pouring from it.

"Don't breathe the smoke!" he said. "And repeat after me, 'Maman Sanite, Queen of the Villeres, as blood of your blood and son of your kin, I pray to the Loa to end your terror reign. Get thee to Guinee where forever you'll stay.'"

They repeated the chant. "Again!" They said it together this time. Headless Zonbi Grisé was on its foot and peg leg and coming for them. "Once more. As loud as you can!"

"Maman Sanite, Queen of the Villeres, as blood of your blood and son of your kin, I pray to the Loa to end your terror reign. Get thee to Guinee where forever you'll stay!"

Black smoke darkened the brightness of the flames, coating them with putrid hate. Julien struggled to keep from inhaling, and with the last "stay," he threw the blood-stained Voodoo doll into the fire, praying the insight Samedi had granted him was correct.

The fire flared up one final time before being sucked down into the earth in a churning black hole. The vortex opened further, the wind increasing as the black smoke followed the flames with an inhuman shriek. As soon as the tail end of the smoke was pulled underground, the hole closed up.

Zonbi Grisé crumpled into a pile of bones and flesh and tattered fabric. Quiet darkness blanketed the clearing, bringing with it a strange sense of calm and peace.

CHAPTER TWENTY-TWO

With far more emotion than she was capable of processing, Nichole watched Julien limp around the cleared fire circle. He checked on Norbert, who was still slumped and presumably unconscious, tested Brigitte's restraints and gag, tried to power on his phone not once, but three times, mouthing "fuck" each time the phone refused to comply, scattered more dirt on the extinguished fire, and retrieved a backpack before finally joining her on the makeshift bench she shared with Daddy.

She watched his hands reach for hers. "The phone is dead," he said as he wrapped her fingers in his. "No point in even trying. I called the cops earlier. Hopefully that'll be enough to get them here."

She nodded, unsure of what to say next. She focused on the strength of his touch. He'd taken care of so much. He was taking care of so much. He'd rescued her, he'd saved her, he'd been her rock when no one else was there... How could she possibly convey her gratitude? She could barely talk.

"You okay?"

She lifted her head to look at him, grimacing with the effort. Her entire body ached from the pain of constant muscle strain. But she was more than okay. He was here. Daddy was here. She couldn't ask for any more.

She managed to nod. Her brain sloshing around in her skull only intensified the throbbing between her eyes. It definitely didn't help the nauseous pit growing in her stomach, either.

"Here." Julien handed her a warm bottle of water. It felt amazing sliding down her raw throat and she nearly drank it all in one gulp, making the nausea worse. Her hand flew to her mouth and she closed her eyes, fighting the urge to barf.

"Careful, try to drink more slowly. You've got to be seriously dehydrated."

"Now you tell me," she rasped.

Their eyes met and she was reminded just how amazingly green his were. For a split second, she found it difficult not to get lost in them. She looked away, remembering nothing was certain with Julien, and if the desert in her throat was any indication, Daddy must be dying of thirst.

Sitting beside her, his head hung heavily on his shoulders as he stared at the bloody blisters on his hand. She twisted toward him and held out the water bottle out. Her hand shook like the thing weighed thirty pounds instead of three ounces. Julien immediately jumped up and took the bottle from her, carefully helping her father take a sip. He managed a few tiny swallows before pulling his head back with a shake. A sad, trembling smile cracked the corners of his lips. Julien nodded in understanding and Daddy went back to staring at his hands. It broke her swollen heart.

"I wasn't sure I'd ever see him again," she whispered when Julien rejoined her.

"I know." His arm wrapped around her shoulder, bringing her closer to him. It felt good and she closed her eyes when he kissed her hair.

It was time she said something, *anything* to let him know how she felt. "Thanks for the shirt," was what she came up with. "It smells like you, maybe with a touch of B.O."

"You don't exactly smell like roses, sister." He pulled her in tighter. "Kind of a mix of swamp, Bourbon Street, and fabric softener. I can't say I hate it."

She caught the movement of his lips when they rose and knew he was teasing. Once again, his inappropriate jokes really did help ease the tension.

"So, what happens next?" she murmured after a minute.

"Well," he started, "the police will probably want a statement from you and your father, and then..."

"No," she interrupted. "I mean..." Her lips pursed together. She really sucked at this. Not that relationships had even been her specialty.

"Your necklace is gone," he said casually, like he hadn't heard the quiver and uncertainty in her voice. "Are the voices back?"

She wasn't sure why he'd suddenly bring that up. He must not want to discuss their future…them. She didn't blame him, and she certainly wouldn't blame him if the only thing he left behind once the police arrived were skid marks. "No. I don't think they wanted anything to do with that…curse."

"Probably not. Don't worry though, I'll put together a nicer one for you once I get back to the shop. We have some beautiful vials you can fill with salt. It's probably a good idea for one to become part of your wardrobe."

It took a moment for his words to register. Once they did, it dawned on her. It wasn't that he didn't want to discuss their future, but he was diverting the conversation and once again easing her tension.

The faint sound of sirens sounded in the distance. She felt Julien relax beside her.

"Thank God," he said quietly. "Looks like our escort will be arriving soon."

They sat in silence for a moment and as content as she was to linger in his embrace, she knew she still needed to find out. To ask the hard question.

He beat her to it. "So are you headed back to Baton Rouge after this is all smoothed over?"

"Not right away. I think I should stay and make sure Daddy is…recovered before I head home."

He nodded. "Probably a good idea."

The sirens were getting louder, their obnoxious squeal like the most beautiful Mozart serenade, promising safety and a shower.

"And you? Do you think you have enough information for your book?"

He glanced toward Brigitte and Norbert Villere. Norbert was still passed out. Brigitte was chewing against her gag and shooting ice daggers their way. "Yes, I do. And I think I'm ready to end that chapter of my life." He turned to her. "And start a new one.

You know, Baton Rouge isn't that far from New Orleans."

She smiled against the tears lumped in her throat. "No, it isn't."

EPILOGUE

Glancing down at her watch for the fourth time, Nichole silently cursed herself. Running twenty minutes late for Julien's book signing was absolutely not part of her plan and she hated breaking a promise. Especially when it involved the man she loved. Sure, the accident on the freeway was a big factor, but she should have given herself more time.

Finding a parking spot in the French Quarter on a Saturday night was quite possibly the most difficult task in the universe. And unfortunately, the Villere House of Voodoo was smack dab in the middle of the Quarter.

She'd circled the block six times and was resolved to start looking in Treme and walk the mile to the shop, when the smallest parallel parking space in existence opened up. She may have rubbed bumpers with the neighboring cars, but with more than a few tries, finally squeezed into it.

A line leading to the front door was wrapped around the building, and inside, the small store was swarming with people. As far as she could tell, there was no getting through that crowd.

Luckily for her, she knew another way in and punched the code to unlock the gate leading to back courtyard, quickly stepping into the narrow alley before shutting the gate behind. The back door was wide open, spilling out sounds of chatter, and laughter, and faint music. And from the looks of it, even people. Through the window she could see the place was packed to the hilt with people. Not just in the store, but it was elbow-to-elbow all the way to the living room.

Wow, pretty great turn out.

Wendell stood outside, standing guard like a weathered old sentry. Well, a weathered old sentry drinking a beer.

"Is something wrong? Why are you standing out here alone?"

"Have you gotten a look at that fire hazard in there?" His chin jutted toward the house. "I felt like a cow in a damn feedlot."

She smiled. "It is crowded."

"Well, can't deny that boy wrote a fine book. Ain't no doubtin' why it's popular. Though I can't say I love all the subject matter…"

"I know." She took his hand in hers and squeezed. "I do wish Miss Puts were here," she whispered.

"Well darlin', you know she ain't so keen with tarnish on the Grisé name."

"I do. But it's ancient history. Besides, what family doesn't have a few skeletons in their closet?"

"Or in jail?" Wendell snorted. "D'ya hear the Swamp Villeres got twenty-five years each for all them drugs they were producing?"

Nichole nodded. The details of hers, Daddy's, and poor Claude's kidnapping, so to speak, was so bizarre, they'd decided to limit the charges to producing Meth. There was plenty of condemning evidence, and the sentencing certainly reflected that.

"Don't worry, Nikki," Wendell added. "Ruby is a proud old woman, but she'll come around soon enough."

"I hope so." As irritating a Puts' busy-bodying could be, Nichole knew she meant well. Somewhere deep, deep down below all the fakery.

Leaving Wendell at his guard post, she started the daunting task of making her way through the crowded shop. Attempting to politely snake through groups of chatting people holding glasses of wine, beer, hors d'oeuvres, or all three, she had to apologize when her purse abruptly brushed against a woman's ass—twice. If she thought the house felt small before, this was making it nearly unbearable.

Someone tugged her arm. "There you are." Lottie's tone wasn't accusatory, just relieved. "Come with me. You'll never get through this way."

Lottie pulled her through the crowd and into the back kitchen entrance. Of course, cutting through the kitchen would be the quickest way to the parlor where Julien would be. Nichole had been to the house many times, but the multiple doors and entrances always seemed like a maze.

Standing in the doorway just outside the parlor, Nichole scanned the room until she spotted him, sitting at a small table stacked with books. Julien seemed to notice her immediately, his face brightening as a grin slid across his full lips.

That was all she needed to ease her anxiety. His simple gesture spoke volumes in a crowded room where she could barely hear her own thoughts.

Standing to his left, Daddy and Delia looked quite chummy, taking turns whispering in each other's ears. Daddy had gained all the weight he lost within a month of being freed from his Zonbi prison, but it wasn't until he met Julien's mom that the haunted look left his eyes and *life* returned to his face. They seemed to understand each other much the same way Julien had always *gotten* Nichole. She knew just how unbelievable a feeling that could be, and she loved seeing Daddy so happy. Finally.

"Can you believe this turn-out?" Lottie said.

"Yeah, it's kind of overwhelming."

"It is. I'm just glad we'll have a few days off before Thanksgiving." Lottie said as she took a sip from her glass. "One event down. One to go."

"I'll help you with that. Well, I'll try anyway. I have no idea how to cook a turkey."

"We'll learn together." Shay walked by and Lottie plucked a glass of champagne from his server tray, handing it to Nichole. "Oh, the reno is done on the master suite upstairs."

"Master suite?" From what Nichole remembered, like most historical houses, the upstairs was carved into many small bedroom all sharing a single bathroom.

Lottie looked surprised. "Julien didn't tell you?"

"No…"

"Oh, shoot. It was probably supposed to be a surprise." Lottie sighed. "Well, I guess the cat's out of the bag now. We knocked out the wall between

Grandmere's old bedroom and Xavier's, and added a fabulous en suite. You're going to love it!"

"What about Xavier?"

Lottie wagged her eyebrows. "We found a great little apartment just down the street. Finally. It's taken forever."

"So you're leaving? I hope me moving here isn't forcing you out…"

"No! Not at all. We just thought, well, with everything, it was best that you and Julien stay here and we give you some space. I actually always planned on having my own place, it just kept falling through. It's even better now because I get the added bonus of having Xavier living with me."

"Thanks," Nichole said, giving her a quick sideways hug. "That was really sweet of you."

Lottie hugged her back. "Of course! Hey, Julien is looking a bit anxious. I'm pretty sure he's itching to see you." She nodded to the opposite side of the room.

Nichole looked toward the signing table, and just as Lottie described, Julien's gaze was locked on them even as he scribbled words on the inside cover of an open book.

"I better go."

Not worrying this time how often her purse groped strangers, Nichole pushed her way through the crowd blocking the fifteen feet separating them. Julien rose the moment she was near, stepping from behind the table to embrace her. Wrapping his arms securely around her waist, he kissed her gently, his tongue tasting of champagne.

"God, it's good to see you."

Resting her head on his shoulder, she closed her eyes and knew without a doubt she was home. Home where she was surrounded by people who didn't judge but actually understood her. This two-story, antique house where parking sucked, and drunk tourists stumbled down the streets at all hours of the day and night, was home…and it was where she wanted to be. For the rest of her life.

Blood of My Blood Series
Villere House: **Blood of My Blood**
Book One
Bayou Grisé: **Sins of Sanite**
Book Two

Other Books by C.D. Hussey

The Human Vampire Series
La Luxure: **Discover Your Blood Lust**
Book One
de Sang: **Embrace Your Blood Lust**
Book Two
Eveillez: **Deny Your Blood Lust**
Book Three
Expiez: **Redeem Your Blood Lust**
Book Four

Contemporary Romance
Unexpected Oasis

To stay updated with C.D. Hussey, please visit:
http://www.cdhussey.com/

If you would like stay connected with Leslie Fear, below are a few links to her social media pages:
https://www.facebook.com/author.leslie.fear
https://www.goodreads.com/author/show/7202737.Leslie_Fear
http://www.theindiebookshelf.com/search/label/leslie%20fear
http://jilliandodd.net/category/leslies-book-bliss

ACKNOWLEDGMENTS

A huge THANK YOU to our beta readers: Melanie Pethel, Shannon McCrimmon, Laura Wilson, Beth Rustenhaven, Christy Baldwin, Vanessa Proehl, Sarah Phelps, Tami Fairly, Tashia Brandenburg, Cynthia Perez, Chelcie Holguin, Beth Suit, Shawn Verdin, and Sue Colburn.

ABOUT THE AUTHORS

When not writing, C.D. Hussey enjoys a career as a professional engineer. She currently lives in the Midwest with her husband, teenage son and two cats. With an ongoing love affair with New Orleans, expect to see her in the Crescent City at least twice a year.

Leslie Fear began writing as a stay-at-home-mom and has two unfinished novels she'd like to return to someday. In addition, her love for reading lead to reviewing books for Goodreads and Amazon and also co-founding The Indie Bookshelf blog. She also enjoys her work as review contributor for author, Jillian Dodd's blog.

Leslie lives in Texas with her husband, teenage son and daughter and one very silly pug.

Made in the USA
Charleston, SC
29 October 2015